*Then There was Max*

By
Rise Shapiro

To my mother, my friend
Rehel,
Whose encouragement was endless
With all my love and gratitude

# Acknowledgments

The author's special thanks to:

My darling husband, Alan, who stopped whatever he was doing to help me, whenever I was ready to throw the computer through the window.

My wonderful daughter, Rachel, for going into my file and reading my manuscript, without my knowledge. But then saying she liked it.

My fabulous son, Evan, whose encouraging words were always so helpful.

My parents, sister and brother, who I can always count on to be there when I need them.

"Hello," a tentative whisper sounded on the answering machine. I leaned forward anxiously. It was the voice of a young girl. I knew that voice.

"Hello, Robin?" I sat bolt upright. The whisper continued. "Robin Max needs you, help him. I can't, I tried but...." The receiver clicked and the dial tone buzzed loudly. I sat frozen with fear. What would make her call me and why did she hang up? My thoughts spiral, I wanted to run to Max, grab him and keep on running. I got as far as the door when familiar faces began flashing in my mind, my mothers, my fathers, Jill's and finally David's. I closed my eyes, heart sinking as reality engulfed me. I am as trapped as Max.

## Chapter 1

Gently, I pulled off the dead leaf that hung limply on the geranium. I crushed the leaf in my hand, and dropped it onto the greenhouse floor. I looked the plant over, checked for weeds and fungus, and softly touched the soil. I took a moment and inhaled deeply. I love the smell and gritty feel of loose, dry soil. Weeds had sprouted in the pot of zinnias. Carefully, I pulled out these next.

I wondered what time David would be getting home. He had been coming home late since his promotion as one of the vice-presidents at the bank. Poor nine-to-five David needed to make adjustments. I should make him something special for dinner, maybe that Beef Wellington he loved so much when we had dinner at his parents' the week before. I could call Suzanne for the recipe. I pushed my hair out of my eyes. I should have cut this hair off; I thought angrily, light blond strands falling into my eyes again, but David would have been furious. He loves my hair long, down to my waist so he can twist his hands through it. He was angry enough when I just trimmed my bangs two months ago. Now what was I thinking? Oh, that's right, dinner.

I looked down over my terrace garden. Hundreds of people walked in the busy Manhattan Street below. I watched as they walked out into a sun only beginning to redden. I told myself it was early enough to call Suzanne for that recipe. As I turned to go inside, I noticed my herbs out of the corner of my eye. "Oh look at the herbs!" I exclaimed aloud to no one. "You have all decided to sprout at once." Forgetting Suzanne and the recipe, I quickly returned to my gardening, and spoke happily to my herbs. The reddened sun slowly sank below the horizon.

Absorbed as I was, I didn't hear the French door as it quietly opened, but I felt the hairs on the back of my neck rise, and sensed I wasn't alone. I began to turn, when an arm grabbed me from behind. Screaming, I turned hard until I was completely turned around. I saw a tall slim man, with golden blond hair brushed smoothly back, and very angry green eyes.

"David!" I screamed again. "What are you trying to do, scare me death?"

"Better me than someone doing more than scaring you!" he yelled back. His eyes flashed green. "I can't believe you left the front door unlocked again. How many times have I told you to keep that door locked?" His voice rose until his last words were a screaming crescendo.

"David, you know perfectly well Bill wouldn't let anyone into the building that doesn't live here." My voice shook, not from fear of attackers, but from David's yelling. Bill was the doorman, and I felt perfectly safe with him guarding the front entrance.

"You rely too much on Bill. It takes only a second for someone to slip in the door," David snapped, still glaring at me.

I put down the trowel I held, and put my arms around David's neck and softly kissed him.

"Please don't be angry," I said quietly, as I softly kissed his neck. I kissed his smooth cheek and his strong lips, still pressed tightly together. Softly, I caressed the back of David's thick hair, as I slowly pulled back and looked into his eyes. His eyes had softened and returned to their original hazel.

"How can I stay angry with you when you look at me with those emerald eyes of yours?" David breathed out hard. He rubbed his fingers briskly through his hair, "Damn it! I just don't want anything to happen, to you."

"It won't, David. I promise I'll be more careful. I'll lock the front door at all times." I raised my hand in the Girl Scout promise and smiled. David grunted ruefully. I tried to change the subject.

"Look, David, my herbs have sprouted. Soon, we'll have fresh chives for your baked potatoes!"

"Well, that's sounds good. Speaking of baked potatoes, what's on tonight's dinner menu?"

"Uh, dinner?" I started biting my thumbnail. "Uh, hmm."

"No dinner, again?"

"No, no, I can think of something ," I said, as David put his arm around my shoulder, and we walked inside.

"Have you been out here all day?" David asked.

"No," I replied. "This morning I polished the silver in the china cabinet."

"Robin, we have a cleaning woman to do that. Why the hell are you doing it?"

"She doesn't clean it well. It was my grandmother's. I want to keep it looking nice."

"Find someone that will clean it well!"

"David, I couldn't do that! You know Anne is the sole support of her family. She has two little girls to provide for, and her husband has that slight problem with alcohol."

"There's a name for that, Robin," David said, sounding sarcastic, "the guy's a drunk."

"I can't replace her ," I said ignoring his tone.

"Fine!" David snapped. "At least she keeps the rest of the house clean."

"Yes, she does," I didn't mention the time I helped Anne dust. "Do you mind if I take a shower before making dinner?" I asked.

"No, Robbie, go ahead, I'll change and have some wine."

David took off his suit and put on a light blue shirt and khaki Dockers, poured some wine, and began sorting through the mail. I emerged a few minutes later from the shower in clingy black leggings and a red T-shirt. I pulled my hair away from my face, as I walked out of the bedroom and into the kitchen.

"I guess I should have gone grocery shopping today," I said out loud to myself. David peered over my shoulder and looked into the opened refrigerator. He quickly glanced at the two bottles of water, half container of yogurt and loaf of bread.

"I guess so," he said casually. Then he sternly added, eyes narrowing. "Did you eat today?" I sometimes forget to eat when I'm absorbed in something.

9

"Hmmm uh," I said, shifting on my feet, knowing I was going to hear another lecture.

"Robin, I can't believe…"

"Wait! I had some crackers earlier, does that count?" I said, smiling.

David smiled back as his arms slowly glided down my back, and circled my slim waist, stopped and rested on my bottom.

"Besides, I didn't hear you complain last night on how I looked or felt ," I said as I looked into David's eyes, and tried for a saucy smirk. He laughed and smacked my bottom.

"It's not the way you look or feel that's my concern; I just want to make sure you have the stamina to keep up with me."

I playfully pushed him away from me. He turned towards me, a luminous blue overtaking the green in his eyes as it always did when he was aroused. Then he grabbed me forcefully. A look of possession came over his face. He carried me toward the bedroom.

"Dinner can wait," he said huskily.


After making love, I snuggled my head against David's shoulder. "I love you," I whispered.

"I think you have put some kind of spell on me, Mrs. Pierson. You would think after four years of marriage, I'd stop lusting after you like some damn teenager. When I look at you..." David's eyes slowly traveled from my hair, down to my toes. Dinner was put off again.


We laid in each other's arms. David gently pulled his arm from around my neck, stretched, and rolled to his side of the king-size bed. He took his day planner off the night table and began to flip through it, looking for his last notes.

"What's wrong?" I asked.

"Nothing, I just remembered some information I need for a meeting tomorrow. I want to check these notes to make sure I have everything set.

"Hungry?" I asked. David nodded.

"I'll go order pizza. What do you want on it?"

"Oh, uh, whatever you want ," he answered absently, while reading his notes. I grabbed my pink, silk robe and walked into the kitchen. The light flickered for a moment then brightly lit up the interior. My eyes looked past the granite counter tops with various hardly used appliances scattered about, and fell on my fern. *Poor little fern,* I thought, as I lightly touched its delicate leaf. *I shouldn't have left you on the terrace table; the sun was stronger than I thought. I'll need to keep an eye on you tonight. I'll keep you inside with me.*

I reached for the phone and pressed the speed dial for our favorite pizza place, as I gently caressed my fern's tender leaves.

"Theresa's Pizza. May I help you?"

"Hi, Frank, this is Robin Pierson."

"Mrs. Pierson! How are you tonight?" Frank answered happily.

"Fine, Frank. How is Theresa and the baby?"

"Fine, just fine. And what can I get for you tonight?"

"Oh, uh a small, no better make that a medium, pepperoni pizza. Do you have that cheese bread David loves so much?"

"Sure do! Should I send some over?"

"Yes. Please do."

"You got it. Anything else?"

"No, that's it."

"I'll send Joey right out with your order. It will be there in about thirty minutes."

I hung up the phone and poured some wine into a glass. I leaned on the counter and looked dreamily into the living room. I stared into the fire, in the stone fireplace. David must have lit it while I was in the shower. The firelight reflected off the cream leather sofa, matching wing chairs, and glass coffee table. The white carpet looked soft and inviting in the fire's light. I looked at the Renoir painting hanging over the fireplace. I remembered when we saw it in Paris. I fell in love with it instantly. All the flowers and that beautiful flowing river. David bought it immediately. He said he always wanted a Renoir over the fireplace. On the mantel was the sculpture that David had found in a gallery in Florence. David has such wonderful taste.

I glanced at the stain glass that hangs in the dining room. It makes the glass dining room table and matching china hutch look exquisite. David's footsteps interrupted my thoughts as he came into the kitchen.

He was reading some pages he had in his hand, as he walked toward me. He had put on his red, silk robe and slippers. David hated to go barefoot at any time.

"What were you doing?" I asked.

"Checking up on some of our stocks, Ben gave me a tip on a new company that makes a type of software that is going to be almost obligatory on some of the higher functioning computers in the near future. I think I'll get some shares before the company goes public." My eyes began to glaze over. "Robbie, pay attention! You need to be informed."

"Why? You know what you're doing, or you seem to anyway ," I replied. David knew I barely could follow what he was saying when he talked stocks and trading. I know that David is a smart investor. He knows how to jump on hot stocks.

"I always know what I'm doing ," David said, smiling. "But that doesn't mean you shouldn't know about the stock market."

"I ordered the pizza." David rolled his eyes, definitely noticing my attempt at changing the subject. I thought another stock remark was about to happen, but, instead, his eyes fell upon the fern.

"What is that thing doing in here! I built a ten-thousand-dollar greenhouse for you so I wouldn't have to have these plants in my home. Didn't I tell you that the last time you brought a plant in here?"

"I know, David, but this is a baby. Look, his leaves are brown from too much exposure to the sun today. Just let me keep it here overnight. I'll take it back in the morning, I promise. Please David?"

"All right," he grumbled. "But I want it back in the greenhouse tomorrow. Remember, Robin, we had an agreement that if I had a greenhouse built, you would keep your plants in it, and no leaves on the counter. Who knows what kind of bugs are in that thing?" He grumbled again. "Tomorrow, get rid of it before I get home from work, understand?"

"Of course, David. Let me pour you some more wine." The buzz of the intercom interrupted, and David went to answer it.

"Yes?"

"Pizza delivery for you, Mr. Pierson," said Bill the doorman.

"Thanks, Bill, send him up."

A minute later there was a knock on the door.

"Hi, Mr. Pierson," said Joey.

"Hi Joey," I called from the kitchen. "How are you tonight?"

"Fine, Mrs. Pierson, how's the plants?"

"Fine, except for my poor fern, it got a bit sunburned today."

"That's too bad. If anyone can help the fern, you can, Mrs. Pierson."

"Thanks, Joey ," I said. David gave an exasperated sigh and paid Joey.

"Bye, Mr. Pierson, bye, Mrs. Pierson."

"Wait, Joey," I called. "l have these clippings for Theresa. Please be sure to give them to her."

"I will."

"Bye, Joey."

"Such a sweet boy," I said to David. "Did you give him a nice tip?"

"I gave him the appropriate amount. Come and eat, Robin, I want to know you have eaten at least one meal today."

"Yes, David," I smiled, and joined him at the table.

## Chapter 2

My hand reached absently up to my neck. An annoying, wet tickling feeling kept bothering me. I tried to brush it away with my hand, but it kept coming back. I kept my eyes shut and I tried to ignore the feeling, and return to a deeper sleep. It kept waking me. I grimaced and rolled over onto my back. Then I heard laughter, as if it was far away, and I slowly opened my eyes.

David was sitting beside me, already dressed in his three-piece suit. He leaned over me and kissed the other side of my neck. *So that's what it was,* I thought.

"Sleeping beauty finally decides to awaken," he said smiling. I stretched and yawned.

"You're up early," I replied.

"Up at my usual seven. I'm showered, dressed; breakfast is eaten, and ready for work. What are you doing today, besides lounging in bed?"

"You mean I have to do something else?" I replied as I reached up to smooth back an escaped lock of David's hair.

"Well, no. But if I picture you in bed all day, how will I get through my meetings?"

"I suppose I'll get up after all."

"Do you think you can find time in your busy day to pick up my dry cleaning?" David asked with just a touch of sarcasm.

"I'm sure I can fit that in. Actually, I need to go in that direction anyway. I have some clothes I need to take to the thrift shop."

"What? No!" David interrupted, "I don't want you going there, it's dangerous. All kinds of nasty characters hanging about. And I know you will stop and talk to those people."

"David, they're just people down on their luck."

"I said no, Robin! It's not a safe place for you to go; I'll take you on the weekend."

"You always say that, and then you keep putting it off. Come on, David, I'll take a taxi and I won't talk to anyone, please?"

David agreed reluctantly. "Only if you take a cab. I mean it! No walking. Understand?"

"Yes, David."

"What else are you going to do?" David asked.

"I want to go to Central Park and see my birds. Soon, they will be flying south for winter, lucky birds."

"Do you want to go south, Robbie? I wouldn't mind spending some time on the beach this winter."

"Oh really, David! I would love that."

"I'll look into it. You know Stuart promised me a few days off after this Benson merger. Maybe we can take a long weekend."

"You're lucky to have a boss like Stuart. I guess he's pretty lucky to have you too, David. I know I am."

"Hmm, with flattery like that, I may not even leave for work. Then Stuart won't be too happy with me," he said, as he kissed me. I pulled his head closer to my lips and playfully tickled his teeth with my tongue.

"Robbie, I need to go." David reluctantly moved back and stood up to leave. He turned to me with a stern look. "Remember what I said about being careful at the thrift store. Oh, and take a sweater, it's supposed to get chilly today."

"Yes sir!" I answered, smiling. He laughed and turned to leave. "I love you," I called after him.

"Me, too," he called back. I heard the front door shut and lock securely, as David turned his key in the door from the outside.

I stretched again, and went into the bathroom. I quickly pinned up my hair and filled the Jacuzzi tub. I sprinkled in some of my favorite bubble bath and took a deep breath, Gardenia, I love that smell. I dropped my robe and walked the two steps down into the deep tub. The bubbles swirled around me, exploding into that delicious gardenia scent. I lay back on my bath pillow and closed my eyes, turning off the jets with my feet.

The smell of gardenia made me think of the night David and I met. Gardenias were one of the flowers in my friend Amanda's parents' garden.

We were at their home in upstate New York. They were having a graduation party for Amanda. She had graduated that spring of 1993. I still had a few courses to take that summer to finish my bachelors in Horticulture.

Amanda was excited because her brother, Brett, would be there. He was on holiday from school and he was bringing some of his friends to stay the weekend. Amanda's brother was in his third year at law school and Amanda (as well as her parents) was hoping she and one of Brett's aspiring lawyer friends would hit it off, so to speak. While the maid served drinks downstairs, we were upstairs in Amanda's room finishing our makeup.

"Did you see Brett's friend, the one with the jet black hair and dark blue eyes, Robbie? Wasn't he to die for!" Amanda asked. I wasn't sure which one he was but I answered with an enthusiastic yes. We made our way down to the party, Amanda giggly with excitement. Brett, who knew his role well, called Amanda over.

"Hey, sis, come over and meet my friend, Jeff. I was just telling him about the trip to China we took last summer." Amanda smiled. The giggling was replaced with a look of confidence.

I walked over to the fireplace. I took a glass of champagne off the tray that one of the maids held out to me, and sat down on a Chippendale chair. I self-consciously pulled slightly on the cream-colored silk dress I wore. It was a nice enough summer dress with just a hint of a sleeve and a low-cut bodice, but I felt it was too short.

As I sat, I pulled my feet, encased in pinching high heels, under the chair, my head felt slightly heavy from the weight of my long hair piled high on my head, and my face tight from the heavy make-up Amanda insisted I wear. I lay my head carefully against the back of the chair thinking how I'd rather be in a tank top, shorts, washed face and light lip gloss.

It was too warm for a fire; Amanda's mother had the interior designer put a pinecone arrangement in the fireplace. I was admiring the effect when I heard a soft "Hello" near my ear. I turned and now sitting in the other Chippendale chair was a tall blond man with the most striking hazel eyes I had ever seen. I stared mesmerized, feeling as if I'd fallen into the depths of the ocean, until his smile brought me back. I smiled self-consciously, and looked down at the drink on my lap.

"It's no use trying to hide those emerald eyes," he said, "They're what brought me over to you in the first place. Actually, now that I have an up-close look, there's plenty more to make me stay." I tried to think of a witty reply, but repartee was not my strong suit.

"I'm David, David Pierson," he said. Turning toward him, I extended my hand.

"Robin Stevens," I said, and smiled. David took my hand and squeezed it.

"Are you a friend of Brett's?" I asked.

"Yes," he replied. "I'm in my last year. MBA in finance. Brett and I were roommates during our undergraduate studies. I spent Thanksgiving with these folks."

"Oh," I commented.

"Have you been here before?"

"Oh, yes," I said. "Amanda and I were roommates at school. We did a few weekends. My parents live in Connecticut so it's nice to have Amanda's home as a get-away."

"My parents live in Connecticut too. What does your father do?" David asked.

"He was a cardiologist at Beth Israel Hospital before he retired."

"Is your father the Dr. Stevens that invented that new valve technique for by-pass surgery?" he asked. "

"Yes," I said. "How did you know?" David smiled.

"My father is on the board at the hospital. Dad said the procedure was incredible." I could tell David was definitely impressed. I smiled. I'm very proud of my dad. He was always looking for ways to improve surgical procedures. David glanced out at the arbor where the glow of lanterns gave it a festive air.

"Would you like to walk in the gardens?" David asked.

17

"Yes, I'd love to." That was the beginning.

I smiled dreamily at the remembrance.

David and I saw each other whenever we could after that wonderful night. I finished my degree while David established his career. We married soon after David started at the bank.

I opened my eyes and stared down at my toes and noticed the chipped polish on my big toe. I noticed a chip on the pinky and thumb of my hand. I knew I had better make an appointment for a pedicure and manicure and get it over with. I hate being fussed over at the beauty shop. David likes my nails done well, especially when we have a party to attend. We had an anniversary party for Stuart and Celia the following week. I had to think about buying a new dress too. David will want to go with me. He likes to help pick out my evening clothes. It is fun to go shopping together. David picks out the most beautiful dresses and I get to play model for him. I love dressing up for David.

The water began to chill. I reached for a soft, fluffy towel from the hook and draped it around myself. I walked out of the tub and into the bedroom. I could still smell the gardenia. I pulled on jeans, a light blue T-shirt, and shoes. I pulled the pins out of my hair and quickly ran a brush through it and headed for the kitchen.

I turned on the light and immediately noticed the fern. It looked so much better. "I'll bring you back to the greenhouse so you can be with your friends." I went out the French doors leading to the terrace and carefully carried the fern to the greenhouse door. I placed the fern on a shelf and looked at my herbs, they were beautiful. I plucked a stray weed and turned towards my other plants. Happily, I tended one plant after another.

I glanced down at my wrist, not seeing my watch. I thought I must have forgotten to put it on and wondered what time it could be. I looked up at the sky through the greenhouse roof. The sun was still low. It was around ten or eleven a.m. I told myself, I should start my errands.

I exchanged my sweaty T-shirt for a clean one and went into the kitchen. I looked into the refrigerator for the juice and remembered that we had no food. *Poor David,* I thought, *he must have had dry toast for breakfast.* At least I had coffee for him to make. I saw the coffee in the pot and poured myself a cup.

I added the grocery store to my list of things for the day and thought, about dinner. Having finished the coffee, I went to the closet for the clothes for the thrift shop.

At the lobby, I struggled with the bags of clothes.

"Here, let me help with those bags, Mrs. Pierson, they look too heavy for you to carry."

"Thanks, Bill, would you hail a taxi for me?"

"My pleasure, Mrs. Pierson." The taxi arrived and Bill helped me load the bags.

"Thanks, Bill," I said, as I slid into the taxi's back seat and waved good-bye. I directed the taxi driver and then watched the people as we drove down the busy streets.

So many people all involved in their own worlds. Businessmen dressed in tailored shirts and three-piece suits, holding cell phone conversations and business transactions, which echoed into the air as they walked steadily forward. It was fascinating that no one stumbled, or bumped into one another. Each man knew exactly when to move his arm or side step another person so that no one upset the delicate balance of moving steadily along. They were like mannequins. Machines that never lost their focus. Clear in their destinations. They never noticed the bodies that didn't fit.

I continued to observe. I saw an old man with a ragged beard, mumbling to himself, his ragged shirt stained with tobacco juice. A young woman on a storefront stoop, in a worn housedress. The woman held her infant wrapped in a torn blanket. She seemed to be waiting for someone or something? The cab driver interrupted my thoughts.

"Sorry about the traffic, miss," he said. "There must have been an accident up ahead."

"That's okay, I'm in no hurry," I replied. I waited for him to continue the conversation, but he just turned the volume on the radio up.

I returned to the window. We were close to Central Park, another mile to the thrift shop. I reached into my knapsack. *Oh good,* I thought, *I had remembered the crackers and stale bread for the birds.* I glanced out the window again and saw an older couple shabbily dressed. They were walking slowly towards the park's entrance. Trailing right behind the old couple was a little boy. He looked to be around four years old. The bangs of his blond hair kept falling in his eyes. His dirty hand kept pushing it back. His ragged shirt was torn in several places. His jeans had holes in the knees. He stopped to try to fix the shoelace that he had already stumbled over. The old man turned around and screamed loudly, "Hurry up!" He was so loud that even I could hear him from the taxi. The boy jumped up and moved quickly to the old man's side. The cab driver interrupted again.

"Well, we seem to be moving again," he said.

"Oh good," I said absently. I turned from the window, looked straight ahead and wondered if the boy was their grandson. They seemed too old to be parents. My thoughts quickly faded as I looked out the right-side window, as we pulled up to the curb of the thrift shop.

"Please wait," I said to the cab driver, I began to carry the bags into the store when a goodwill volunteer met me half-way, and helped with my bags.

"Good morning, Mrs. Pierson, thanks for the donation."

"You're welcome, Chris, glad to help, have a good day."

"You too, " Chris called, as he turned around to carry the last of the bags into the store.

I walked back to the waiting cab.

"Please, can you spare some change?" an old woman asked as she approached me. I remembered what David had said about talking to people who loitered there. I began to shake my head, and then I stopped and looked at her. Who did she remind me of? Oh yes, that woman heading toward Central Park with the little boy. I stared at her, wondering if she had a little boy? Or maybe girls? She looked at me uneasily as I stared.

She started to back away. I came out of my trance. I quickly pulled a ten-dollar bill out of my knapsack and gave it to her, without speaking. She grabbed the money and smiled, displaying several missing teeth.

"Bless you," she said, and walked quickly away. I paused, just a second, then ran to the cab and got in.

"Central Park, please," I said to the cabby, a little breathlessly.

"Sure, miss. You know, you shouldn't have given that old lady money. She'll just drink it up." I ignored him.

The cab pulled up to the entrance of the park. I got out and paid the driver. I watched as he pulled away from the curb and flowed into the traffic. I turned and walked into the park. I buttoned my sweater as I walked forward, taking my usual path past the duck pond and over the hill. The fall leaves fell around me, fluttering in a blaze of color. I listened to the crunch of leaves beneath my feet. I watched as my feet scattered the leaves to the sides of the walk. Already, piles of leaves were stacked, they gave the impression of walking by a red, and gold mountain.

I sat on the hill for a few minutes and watched the ducks in the duck pond. The ducks were late this year; usually they were gone by early September. *Must be the stragglers,* I thought.

Joggers, wearing sweatpants, and T-shirts ran on the walk below the hill, sweat glistened on their faces and their shirt fronts, even with the chill in the air. I hugged my arms closer. Impulsively, I ran down the hill, the wind blowing in my face. On the path below, I slowed to a walk. I reached a bench and stopped to straighten my knapsack. I didn't usually come into this area. It was too close to the playground and the children's loud screams scared the birds.

I stood by the bench to straighten the twisted knapsack, and then returned it to my back. I was ready to leave to go to my usual bench, when I saw him. He was the same little boy that I had seen from the cab.

He was climbing on the monkey bars. I sat down to watch him climb. Swiftly, moving like a monkey, he was at the top of the bars. He stood on the top rail and began to walk on the bar like a tightrope walker. I felt myself tense as I watched him. I looked around for the old couple he had come with. The couple sat on a bench across from the monkey bars. The old man was sleeping. The old woman stared into space, occasionally reaching down to pop a cracker or something into her mouth. My gaze went back to the little boy. He had now crossed one bar and was rounding the corner of the next. The corner was tricky and he almost lost his balance. His arms flapped as if he were ready to take flight. I felt myself ready to jump up, to run to him. Easily, he put his hands down and swung himself to the lower bar. He laughed as he grabbed the bar across from him and jumped lightly to his feet.

I took a deep breath. Sweat trickled down my neck and my back. I put my hand over my heart and felt it slowly resume its normal pace. *What was wrong with me?* I asked myself. The kid was just playing. I stood up and walked toward the other side of the park.

As I walked, I glanced back and saw the boy had entered the sandbox. He was now making a fort out of sticks and rocks. At that moment, he looked up and caught my eye. He stared at me. He had hazel eyes. He abruptly turned away, back to his fort, adding more rocks around the sticks, to better defend his fortress.

I walked to my usual bench and sat down. Even before I could get out the bread, birds started landing before me. I smiled at them. *You're nothing if not dependable,* I thought. I threw out some crumbs and crackers. I nibbled on a cracker as I watched the greedy birds pushing one another. "Come now, there's plenty for all of you. " I scolded. "Someone would think you've never eaten."

The sun was warm in this spot and I pulled up the sleeves on my sweater. I glanced at my watch. Two o'clock already. I looked at the trees. I loved the fall, but winter, that I didn't love. I leaned back on the bench and closed my eyes, enjoying the sun on my face. Too soon it would be too cold for the birds, and they would all fly south.

As would David and I. Excitement flooded me. I loved Florida beaches. Especially Sanibel Island. I hoped David would want to stay in one of the resorts on Sanibel. I could envision us as we lay on the beach, or as we danced in one of the many clubs. Or go listen to jazz, or a reggae band. I saw us taking a moonlight cruise. Of course, I would have to talk David into the cruise part. "It doesn't matter," I told myself. "I'm just glad we're going."

David is too good to me; I should do something special for him tonight. Especially since he had that big meeting today, the one he was so concerned about. I would make him a special dinner, with candles and his favorite wine. "Squawk! Squawk!" I opened my eyes to see a flock of angry birds yelling at me. "Okay, I'm sorry," I said, as I threw out the rest of the bread. "That's it, guys, no use complaining, that's all the bread I brought."

I got up and brushed the crumbs off of my jeans. I grabbed my knapsack and headed toward the park entrance, planning tonight's menu leaving the shouts of playing children behind me.

I hailed a cab and had him take me to the grocery store. I decided on fish. David loves trout cooked in white wine. I added rice pilaf and some salad, that would work. I picked up the other foods we needed and told Sam, who delivered the groceries, to bring them to my apartment in an hour.

I went next door to the bakery. I watched a little girl enjoy a cookie as I waited for my turn. She chewed each bite slowly and smiled with the joy the taste brought her. Her mother looked down at her daughter's chocolate face, took a bit of tissue from her purse, and carefully wiped the girl's mouth.

Other children munched cookies while mothers decided on baked goods. A mother played with her daughter's hair. Another occupied her son with patty cake as she patiently waited her turn. I thought about the little boy at the park, the one with the hazel eyes. Though I knew better, I asked myself who fed him cookies and lovingly wiped the cookie crumbs from his face. Did someone ever play patty cake with his little baby hands?

"Number 22," the lady behind the counter called out. I handed her my ticket.

"I'd like a French bread, please, not sliced.," I said hurriedly. She carefully slipped my bread into its paper bag and handed it over the counter.

"Anything else?"

"No, thank you. Wait, yes, I'd like a dozen chocolate chip cookies also." *What am I doing?* I thought, as I walked out of the bakery, *David and I don't eat cookies! The Donaldsons on the first floor,* I told myself. *I'll give the cookies to them.* I was close friends with Paula Donaldson. She didn't mind if I gave the kids sweets now and then. Paula teased me that my mommy hormones were beginning to surface.

I stopped at the dry cleaners, and hailed a taxi to take me the two blocks home.

"Let me help with all those things, Mrs. Pierson," Bill said.

"Thanks, Bill. My groceries should be coming soon. I bought these treats for the Donaldson children. Would you give the cookies to them for me?"

"Sure thing, Mrs. Pierson, you sure spoil those boys."

"It's nothing," I said, as I went into the elevator. *At least some little boys will be eating cookies tonight,* I thought.

I set the bread onto the counter, and hung up David's clothes. The buzzer rang,

"Yes, Bill?"

"Your groceries are here, Mrs. Pierson."

"Thanks. Send them up."

The groceries delivered, I carefully put things away as I listened to my messages on the answering machine. Beep. "Robin, it's Jill, I'm hoping we can do lunch tomorrow, I have a stunning new dress for the party next week that I want to tell you about. Call me!" Oh good. That would be fun.

Lunch with Jill was always fun. Maybe she could give me an idea on a dress to buy.

Beep. "Hi Robbie, it's me, just wanted to let you know I'll be home a half-hour later than usual. Love you."

"Love, you too, David ," I said into the fridge.

Beep. "Hello dears, your father and I are having a wonderful time in Honolulu. We're off to Maui tomorrow. We'll call you from there on Saturday. Love you both." Nice. Glad my parents were having a good time. I couldn't believe they had anything left to see in Hawaii. It was their sixth time to the islands. Mom said that was the only place Dad could truly relax. I took a piece of cheese and went into the living room.

Where was that CD? I felt a little anxious. Bach calmed me down. I sipped a Perrier, as I listened to the soft sounds. I closed my eyes and saw myself floating in the clouds. I learned the technique in meditation class. I relaxed totally. That class was great. Maybe I would take yoga in the spring. The same teacher would be teaching it and she was fabulous.

I looked at my watch. David would be home at six-thirty. Time to cook.

I had just lit the candles on the table when David walked in. His glance took in the lace tablecloth, wineglasses, and fresh flowers from the greenhouse. His look also took in the black, clinging dress, with the spaghetti straps that I wore, his favorite.

"What's this?" he asked, smiling broadly.

"Just a little dinner I whipped up for my hard-working husband, you know, the one I adore," I answered, as I put my arms around his neck and caressed his cheek.

"Hmm," he said, as he began to nibble my earlobe.

"Dinner first tonight, my love," I said, as I took his briefcase and helped him off with his suit coat. "I worked too hard to have it burn."

"Let me change into something more comfortable."

"Okay, I'll pour the wine ," I replied.

Minutes later, David emerged in his silk robe.

"You certainly got comfortable," I said, smiling.

"I'm hoping for a Jacuzzi bath for two later this evening ," he replied, smiling back.

"I think that can be arranged. Here's your wine. To tonight!" I toasted. David raised his glass and sipped his wine, as he sat down.

"Is that your pâté? I love that."

"I know, that's why I made it. How was your day? Did the Benson meeting go okay?"

"Yes, it did," David said around his bite of pate. "We closed the deal today. That's why I was late getting home. Stuart took everyone out for drinks."

"That was nice of him," I replied. I served the fish and rice.

"It's part of being a good businessman. By the way, Stuart said he's looking forward to dancing with you at the anniversary party ," David said smiling. "It's nice to have a beautiful wife to impress the boss with, but he's the only one I want to see you dancing with besides me." David's eyes tensed as his smile faded. He hated it when other men touched me. He tolerated it with friends, but preferred me by his side. I smiled, making light of it.

"Of course, David, who else would I want to dance with except my favorite guy? I'll give the rest of the dances to you ," I said cheekily, as I turned back to the kitchen. He laughed, his face relaxing, as he reached out to smack my bottom.

I laughed as I thought of dancing with chubby, balding Stuart. Stuart was very sweet and very charming, which is probably why his bank was rated number two in Manhattan, but hardly a turn on.

"Why don't I see you eating?" David called into the kitchen.

"Here I am," I said, as I sat down across from him.

"Any calls?" David asked.

"My mom called. My parents are having a great time in the islands. They will call us on Saturday from Maui."

"That's nice ," David said without interest.

"Jill's meeting me for lunch tomorrow. She already bought her new dress for the party."

"And when are you getting a new dress for the party?" David asked.

"Saturday, I hope. You can go with me to pick one out. I love your taste." I could tell from David's expression that this pleased him.

"Of course, I'll choose the dress. I have tennis in the morning with Stuart and Ben. We'll go in the late afternoon and then we can go to that new French restaurant for dinner. Call and make reservations for four and I'll invite Ben and his wife to join us. Stuart already has plans. You better make it for eight o'clock so we have plenty of time to shop," David said.

"Okay," I said. I was not crazy about Ben's wife Joanne, but I knew how fond David was of Ben, so I didn't say anything.

After dinner, David read the journal and sipped brandy in the living room. The dishes done, I went behind him on the sofa and massaged his neck.

"Don't stop," David murmured. "That feels great." He put down the brandy glass and paper, pulled me over the couch onto his lap, and slowly kissed me.

"Now, to our bath." He carried me into the bedroom and slowly undressed me. I kissed him then went to fill the tub.

"No flower scents," he called out. "I enjoy the gardenia smell on you, but not on me."

"No scents," I replied. "How about some bubbles?"

"Bubbles are nice," he called back.

I reached for my unscented bubble bath that I kept just for David. He entered the bathroom and watched me swirling the bubbles.

"Nice view," he said, as he ran his hand over my body. He kissed my shoulder and stepped into the tub. He pulled me on his lap and held me tight as he leaned back on the soft bath pillow. I melted into his shoulder and breathed deeply.

I loved David's smell. I don't think I could have married a man if I didn't like his scent. My sense of smell is heightened by my work with my flowers and plants.

"Penny for your thoughts," David said.

"I'm thinking how much I like the way you smell," I answered. David laughed.

"That is the first time I have ever received that compliment," he said.

I slowly lifted my eyes. He pulled my mouth to his and we melted together into a passionate embrace.

# Chapter 3

1 woke the next morning to the sound of running water. *It must be raining,* I thought sleepily. Then as the fog cleared from my mind, I realized that David was in the shower.

I laid awake in that bliss of just waking, humming to myself.

"Good morning," he said with a sly grin. "I thought you would sleep in after the workout we had last night."

"Ha, ha, I don't see you suffering any ill effects. Why should I?" I asked.

"Well, we both know how fragile you are," he replied mockingly. I threw a pillow at him, which he deftly ducked. I could hear his laughter as he went into the kitchen. *Smarty pants,* I thought.

I could hear the whirl of the coffee grinder. David loved fresh ground coffee. He never went for the flavor craze. He said, "Plain coffee has always been the perfect drink, why change a good thing?" He was pouring orange juice and making toast. I know he would fill the glass exactly three-quarters full and use one teaspoon of marmalade per piece of buttered toast. The only time he deviated from this breakfast was on weekends. On Saturdays, he plays tennis and eats a late brunch at his club and on Sundays, I usually make brunch. He's nothing, if not consistent. I turned over and went back to sleep.

I woke to bright sunlight as it shone through the window. I jumped up, and look at the clock radio, oh good, I sighed with relief, it was just nine-thirty. I wasn't meeting Jill until two o'clock. Jill had an appointment at the hair salon this morning. I threw on some gardening clothes and went to the kitchen for coffee. I carried my cup out to the garden.

As I closed the French door and walked across the terrace toward the greenhouse, I couldn't believe my eyes! I saw lying before the door, a black-capped chickadee! It looked just like the picture in my birding book. I have only seen one other one, once in Central Park. I ran over to it. It was so tiny. It couldn't have been more than four inches long. The chickadee's eyes were closed and his beak stood straight up into the air. I feared the worst. I knelt beside it, put my coffee cup down, and softly touched his wing. He was still warm, a good sign. I looked at his beak and saw blood on it. The blood was close to dry. I looked up and saw blood on the edge of the greenhouse roof, "Oh, poor thing, it must have thought my plants were a good resting spot, and didn't realize the clear roof was glass.

I opened the greenhouse door and took out a clean towel. I gently wrapped it around the bird and picked it up. *Now what?* I thought. *Maybe I should call a vet.* I went back into the apartment and dialed information. They gave me the telephone number of a vet near me. I quickly called. I could feel the heartbeat of the chickadee, steady but fast. I told the receptionist about the bird.

As I was on hold, the chickadee opened its eyes. He took one look at me with his wide, frightened eyes, and tried to back off the counter. Then seeing that he couldn't move, he tried his best to wriggle from the towel. I tried to speak soothingly to him, adding little chirping sounds. The bird sounds seemed to help him relax. The vet's assistant got on the phone and I explained the situation. He told me he thought the bird was just stunned and to put him in a box wrapped in a towel. This way, the bird would think he couldn't get out and he wouldn't try to move. Then he would rest. I should also try to get him to drink some water and give him a little birdseed and he should be fine by tomorrow. I hung up, relieved. I put together a bed, an old shoebox, and put another towel on the bottom. I held the chickadee up, and tried to lower him enough so he could get some water from a bowl that I filled. He didn't want the birdseed, but he did take a little water. Then I gently laid the chickadee inside.

I decided to place him on a corner of the kitchen counter, next to the wall. The bird's eyes were closed again, and his breathing seemed regular. I had never been this close to a wild bird, so I wasn't at all sure what regular breathing should sound like. I decided to change lunch to Monday, since I didn't want to leave the bird alone. What if it tried to fly and fell? I left a message on Jill's answering machine.

I stayed in the house, and didn't work in the garden in case the bird might need me. I didn't feel comfortable leaving it alone.

I kept checking on it and tried several times to give it water and some birdseed. It finally ate a little. I watched it as I made dinner. Its eyes were open and more alert now. He seemed to watch me as well and even tried to turn his head when I walked out of his view.

By the time dinner was in the oven, the bird gave me a chirp.

"Hi. little fellow," I said softly. "Are you ready to talk to me?" I chirped softly to him and he tentatively answered me with his own soft two-note chirp. We were still chatting when David walked in.

David whistled softly, as he entered the apartment. My chickadee friend thought a fellow bird had entered the room and began to whistle back. David froze, and stood staring at the back of the door. He quickly turned around, his hazel eyes huge. They held a stunned expression.

"Hi," I said, smiling hesitantly. David's eyes moved quickly from the bird, the box, to me.

"What is that? And why is it here?" he exploded. His eyes flashed green.

"Well," I began weakly, "It's a bird that I found injured by the greenhouse. It was stunned when it mistook the glass roof for an opening to visit the garden."

"Okay. Now why is it here?" David asked next, a little less loudly than his last question.

"Because, I want to help it, besides it was my greenhouse that caused his accident."

"Birds get hurt all the time, Robin, are you going to bring them all in here to live?" David replied sarcastically.

"No," I said quietly. David was using that mocking tone I dreaded. I took a deep breath to keep my own voice steady. "I felt responsible, since it was my garden he was trying to visit."

"Robin, don't you know that wild birds carry disease! My God!" he yelled truly horrified, "You cooked dinner with that thing in here! Are you nuts! I can see it all now, you probably were so obsessed with the bird that

31

you didn't even wash before cooking my dinner. Didn't you stop and think at all before picking that diseased thing up!"

"David, I thoroughly scrubbed before making dinner. Besides, it isn't diseased, and...."

"How do you know it's not diseased?" David interrupted, still yelling. I took another deep breath.

"I'm around birds at the park enough to know what a sick bird looks like. This chickadee is just stunned, and I want to help it. I called the vet and he agreed with me. The vet said he will be fine by morning. He is already much better than when I found him. I'll just keep him here tonight and then send him on his way tomorrow. See, " I said, as I held my hands up and reached to put my arms around him. "No pox, not even a stray feather." David glared at me.

"You won't just keep him in here tonight," David replied, still yelling and shaking his finger at me. "You'll keep it in the greenhouse, until tomorrow. I don't want any damn animals, much less wild ones in my home. Is that clear?"

David stared angrily into my eyes. I glared back. We continued this for a minute. It seemed much longer. I knew from his eyes he would not be moved on this one. I took the chickadee, box and all, and stalked off to the terrace.

"Fine!" I yelled as I slammed the French door as hard as I could. I gently set the box and bird on one of the greenhouse shelves. The chickadee chirped softly at me, almost seeming to be asking for reassurance against the loud voices and angry words. "Sshh, it's okay," I said, and softly chirped back. I started pulling weeds, thankful for something to release my anger.

The sun was beginning to set when I heard David enter the greenhouse. I was a little calmer now and was replanting a seedling. He walked to me and softly laid his hands on my shoulders.

"I finished dinner," he said quietly, next to my ear. "Will you come eat with me?" I tried to shrug him off but he wouldn't let go. His hold on me felt warm and I could hear the apology in his voice, even though I knew I would never hear the words.

"The bird looks comfortable in here," he said. The chickadee had been singing to me as I worked with my plants.

"I suppose," I said.

"Come," David said, "wash up and I'll have dinner on the table for you." He let go then. I knew if I didn't follow, he would leave and probably get angry again. This was all I would get by way of an apology for his irrational behavior, and was more than I usually got. I put down my spade and checked once more on the chickadee, he would be fine for the night.

David was busy getting dinner on the table. I went and washed up and came back to help him. He smiled at me.

"Stuart put me on a new account today, one that should prove extremely profitable for the company, and maybe us." The bird issue was now closed in David's mind, and I knew not to reopen it.

"Great," I said quietly. David talked on about work, not noticing that I was still upset about the bird.

As he talked, I took a deep breath and smiled at David as we sat down. I told him the arrangements I had made for Saturday night. We didn't refer to the chickadee again.

# Chapter 4

When I opened my eyes the next morning, it was still dark in the room. I looked over to David. He was snoring softly, his head pillowed on his bent arm. His chest rose and fell slowly, keeping a rhythm with his snores. I looked at the clock. Seven o'clock. Since it was Saturday, I knew David would sleep until at least nine.

Yesterday drifted through my mind. I got up, put on my heavy robe, and went to check on my guest in the greenhouse. The October mornings were getting chilly. I could hear flapping. I quickly opened the door and saw a blur speed past my face. Automatically, I ducked as the chickadee landed on one of the shelves. He chirped to me happily.

"And a merry good morning to you, Mr. Chickadee." I walked toward him. He quickly flew to the other side of the greenhouse. "Still not that trusting," I said. "Good, there are too many humans who might hurt you, it's best to keep to your own species."

I continued this one-sided conversation as I laid out a little water and seeds and slowly backed away. As he ate, I went and opened the greenhouse door and sat in my chair. The bird looked at the door and then at me. He cocked his head as if asking what to do next. Then he took one last sip of water and quickly flew out the door. I stood up and watched him go. He landed on the side of the roof, then stopped and gave me one last farewell chirp. *Be well,* I thought, as I watered my plants, not quite ready to go inside yet.

Later, I went back into the kitchen. David had already started coffee. I listened to the coffee maker growl as I watched it slowly drip into the waiting pot. David came and kissed me softly on the cheek. He looked clean and fresh in his white tennis shirt and shorts,

"Won't you be cold in that?" I asked.

"I'll be okay. It's just a short ride to the club, and with the indoor courts, I'll be fine. I have a change of clothes for after we're done playing. I'll be back at two and then we'll go shopping." David was pouring coffee for us both as he talked.

"Great," I replied as I took my cup. David took a few more sips and put his cup in the sink.

"I'm off," he said and kissed me goodbye.

"Bye sweetie, I love you," I called after him.

I finished my coffee and headed into the bathroom for a nice long soak in the tub.

I drifted from one activity to another all morning, not really being able to focus on any one thing. My thoughts were unsettled. I was feeling anxious again, but I wasn't sure why. I always had problems dealing with my emotions. I have a tendency to put them on the back shelf to think about them later. That was the reason I took the meditation class last summer.

I turned on my meditation tape. Slowly, I sat down on the carpet, legs folded, hands resting gently on my knees, palms upward. I took deep breaths and felt myself go into deep relaxation. I took longer than anyone in the class to learn how to totally let myself go, but once I did, the teacher said I could go deeper than any students she had previously taught.

Time holds no meaning during meditation. When I began to resurface, I sensed that it had gotten late. I opened my eyes and David was sitting on the couch, watching me. His eyes held an expression that I didn't see often, one of almost envy.

"I said your name when I came in," he said. "It was almost as if you didn't hear me. You do that so well. I wish I could relax like that."

"I could teach you."

"I don't think I could let go as completely as you do."

"You have other ways of relaxing. How was the tennis game?"

"Great ," David said, as he stood up to go put his racket away.

"That friend of Stuart's was a great tennis player. He really gave Ben and me a workout. I told Ben we would meet them for drinks at seven-thirty tonight. Do you need more time to finish your tape or are you ready to go?"

"Let me change." I slipped on a dress and pumps. "Let's go," I said.

We went down to the parking garage and got into David's Lexus. I'm glad he didn't mind driving in Manhattan. I always preferred taking cabs or walking. We drove to our favorite boutique on Madison Avenue. The shop wasn't crowded, with the exception of one bored husband who kept checking his pocket watch.

"May I help you?" a salesclerk asked.

"Yes," David answered before I could say anything, "My wife is looking for a formal dress for an anniversary party."

"Of course, we have a fine selection to choose from, what size are you?"

"A size two," I answered.

"Please, sit here on the sofa, and I'll bring out a selection of dresses for you to choose from." Once sitting, David leaned back and put his arm around me.

"She sees a nice piece of change coming her way," he whispered, smiling. David loved to be treated well. He has even left places where he felt they were not giving him enough preferential treatment. I smiled. This didn't really bother me, it made me feel special.

The salesclerk returned with her arms loaded.

"This pale yellow will look nice with your skin tone." I went to try it on and then came out to model. When I returned, David was looking, at the other dresses the salesclerk brought out.

"Oh, lovely!" the salesclerk said excitedly.

"Too short," David replied.

"Right, David ," I said.

"Try this rose silk ," David said. It was a long dress, tightly fitting with a slit up to my knees. I liked the way the long sleeves flared at the wrist.

"That's a beautiful choice," the salesclerk stated. I went back in the dressing room and tried it on. I loved the style. It was very flattering.

"You look terrific, Robbie."

"Splendid, just splendid," said the salesclerk.

"I like it too. Let's look at the others before we decide." David sighed, he knew I couldn't make a decision that fast. I tried on three more, but just as David had said, the rose was the nicest. As I emerged from the dressing room, David looked at his watch. He was definitely getting impatient.

"The rose," he said shortly.

"You're right, let's get it."

"Wonderful," said the salesclerk.

David signed for the dress and I went and changed. David had the dress sent. The salesclerk assured me it would be at my apartment by Tuesday morning. We left the shop and decided to walk a bit since it was only shortly past five.

David walked fast, even without a destination. I watched him as he kept his head straight, eyes focused on what was up ahead. He reminded me of the businessmen mannequins I saw from the cab the other day. I went to grab his hand, to assure myself he wasn't a machine. He turned to look at me.

"What?" he said, smiling.

"Nothing, I just wanted to hold your hand." He squeezed my hand.

"We should be getting back," he said. We turned around and walked back to the parking garage. He moved a little slower now, even though his eyes were still focused.

David and I both took showers when we got home. I decided to wear my long-sleeved, cream-colored dress, since it was getting cold. David put on his navy blue suit. I had twisted my hair into a French knot.

"Why don't you wear that tricolor gold necklace we brought back from Milan last summer? That would go well with that dress, and your hair," David said as he kissed my neck.

"Okay," I answered as I went to get it. I held the necklace out to David, and I turned around. He gently put the necklace around my neck. Then he fumbled with the clasp as he began kissing the back of my neck again.

"You smell so nice. It must be a new scent. I would have remembered you wearing this before," he said, mumbling into my ear.

"It is," I said , turning around, and placing my arms around his neck. "I bought it a few weeks ago when I went shopping with Monica. She has wonderful taste in perfumes."

"Oh yes, the perfume authority," David continued as his lips went from my neck to my hair.

"Lately, she's becoming the baby authority," I replied. David shook his head. Monica was due with her first child in early April.

"What was Rob thinking? Christ, they've only been married two years!"

"Not everyone follows your timeline, David." I heard a slight edge to my voice, not sure why it was there. David heard it too.

"What the hell is that supposed to mean? Don't tell me your hormones are kicking in!" David turned from me and roughly yanked his tie into place. I wasn't sure what I was feeling. The anxieties of the day came back. I didn't think it was a baby I wanted, not yet anyway.

"No David," I said, smiling and kissing him gently. "I'm still too busy taking care of you."

"As it should be." He smiled at me and began kissing my neck again.

"Careful, David, that hairstyle took a long time to make."

"If you don't want me to ravish you, you shouldn't make yourself so irresistible ," he teased. I laughed.

"I guess I can redo it ," I said. David looked at me lovingly, then looked at the clock. He sighed.

"No, we can't keep them waiting, come, my love, this will have to keep until later." He grabbed my wrap from the chair where I had laid it, and placed it around my shoulders. I picked up my evening bag and we went down to the car.

The parking lot of the restaurant was crowded. David drove up to the valet parking. He handed the keys to the valet.

"Be careful, don't drive it too fast," David warned.

"Don't worry, sir." I smiled at the valet, he smiled back. I thought he must hear that warning a hundred times a night. David took my arm and we walked into the lounge area.

"Over here, David," Ben called from the corner. We walked over. David smiled and shook Ben's hand. He turned to Joanne.

"How lovely you look tonight," he said as she pecked his cheek. Ben had just said similar greetings to me and I turned to Joanne.

"Robin, you look stunning, and that necklace is breathtaking!" Joanne said. There was a subtle sarcasm to her words that always made me feel uncomfortable, but I knew David didn't hear it.

"I picked that out for Robin when we were in Milan last summer. It does suit her well if I say so myself," David replied, definitely pleased with Joanne's reaction.

"I should have guessed," Joanne said, gushing. Well, at least now she sounded sincere. "Your taste, David, is impeccable," Joanne continued. I smiled, but sighed inwardly, as we sat down. This would be a long evening.

The waiter then came up. I ordered the house red wine that the restaurant was known for. David ordered a vodka martini. David and Ben were quickly engrossed in conversation about the morning's tennis match. Joanne and I discussed fashion and talked about the dresses we bought for the anniversary party. Our drinks came and I slowly sipped the wine. It was delicious. The fragrant bouquet was in itself intoxicating.

Joanne joined into the men's conversation when it turned toward the anniversary party.

"It's amazing what extremes Stuart is going to for this party. You would think it was their fiftieth anniversary instead of their thirty-second," stated Joanne. She was always impressed by a lot of pomp and glitter.

"Celia was very ill last winter. Stuart was almost afraid he would lose her. I'm sure he feels there is a lot to celebrate this year," said Ben.

"Really," Joanne continued, "to rent out the top floor of one of the most beautiful hotels in the city! Extreme! I can't begin to think what that would cost, and the band Stuart hired. It is the most sought after in Manhattan, if not all of New York!"

I took another sip of wine. I had spent a lot of time with Celia when she suffered through pneumonia last winter. A nicer person I have yet to meet. Even when Celia was so ill, her concern was that her charity work would not get done. I tried hard to fill her shoes, and I came home every night exhausted. Joanne was still going on about Stuart's expenditure for the party.

When she paused, I said, "I think Stuart enjoys spending every penny. He is grateful that Celia is still here with him to celebrate this wonderful occasion." Joanne looked at me like I was simple.

"Robin, we all know that."

"Robin spent a lot of time with Celia when she was ill ," David added.

"How wonderful. I wish I had had the time to help Celia." Joanne sighed. "I was just so busy with the cruise plans last spring, and that week I spent at the health spa, impossible!" Joanne was interrupted by the Madre D

"Excuse me, your table is ready." I thankfully stood up to follow him to our table. Once seated, I quickly changed the conversation.

"Ben, David tells me that Stuart has you both working on getting a new jewelry store account." David smiled at me knowingly, and he added his own comments.

We paused in our conversation to study the menu. After I knew what I was ordering, I looked around while the others were still deciding. The place was definitely as beautiful as we were led to believe from all our friends that had been here. There was a gigantic chandelier hanging from the cathedral ceiling. The crystal was gleaming. There must have been a thousand prisms hanging down. Decorative angels were made out of the crystal and circled around the sides of the chandelier. The sides were so wide, it must have taken at least fifty angels to complete the circle. The prisms arced downward and ended in a point, with a lovely crystal hanging from the point. On the ceiling, more angels were painted. Gold columns were evenly spaced around the walls, and gold and silver cloth was hung from each and looped down and up to the next. The walls were painted a soft ivory to accent the gold columns. *How lovely,* I thought, I almost felt as if I was back in Paris in a grand ballroom.

"My goodness!" Joanne exclaimed suddenly. Startled, I jumped and looked at her.

"I almost forgot to tell you about our new addition to the family," Joanne said, as she reached into her purse and pulled out a photo. "Here he is! Isn't he the sweetest thing?" Joanne asked as she passed the photo to me. I looked at the adorable Chitzu puppy and my eyes misted. David glanced over my shoulder at the puppy.

"Ben, I can't believe you'd get a dog. Did he ruin your furniture yet?" Ben laughed. Joanne glared at David.

"Is that all you can say about my precious puppy?"

"Oh, he's very cute, Joanne." David tried to make amends. Joanne was mollified.

"Robin, he is just so adorable! I named him Bitsy because he is such a tiny thing, and you should see how he looks after he has spent the day at the beauty parlor. The cute little blue bows they put in his hair are to die for!" Joanne happily sighed, then looked at me, smirking. "I'm surprised you don't have a dog, Robin, the way you love plants and birds so much."

I thought about the chickadee today. How much fun it would be to have a pet. I opened my mouth to reply.

"The only thing I want warm and cuddly in our apartment is Robin," David interrupted as he put his arm around me and gave me a squeeze. I smiled weakly.

"How sweet," Joanne said with an icy tone.

"To your new addition," I toasted.

"Hear hear," David said, and Joanne smiled.

The waiter came out with our meals. Joanne was complaining about something not coming out right in her order. This was the usual occurrence when we dined with them. I ignored it and turned to take a bite of David's duck. It was delicious. David gave me an exasperated look. I just smiled with my mouth closed. He can't stand sharing his food, but I can never resist trying what he has ordered. Joanne was busy exclaiming to Ben once again, that she can't understand why waiters can never get her order correct the first time.

"So when are you taking the days off that Stuart promised you?" Ben asked as soon as Joanne calmed down.

"Robin and I are planning to go to Florida for the New Year. With that additional time added on to New Year's holiday, we'll have time for a nice vacation."

"What a great idea!"

"Robin hates the cold and it's not my favorite time of year either."

"I hate the cold too, especially in January. Maybe we should go south this winter too, Joanne."

Joanne looked at Ben as if he lost his senses. "What and leave little Bitsy!"

"We can take him with us," Ben said.

"And let him suffocate in one of those little airline crates. Out of the question, Ben. He's still a little puppy, he can't be subjected to all that confusion." Ben just looked at us and sighed. David smiled and sipped his wine.

Smugly he said, "That's why it's important to think these responsibilities through before taking them on. Robin and I have nothing to tie us down. Our housekeeper waters Robin's plants. We're free to go wherever we want, right, Robbie?" David squeezed my shoulder again.

"Yes, David," I said.


"That was fun," David said, as we got into our car and headed home. "That Ben, he's a real go getter at the office, but Joanne rules the roost at that house. She could take some lessons from you on the correct way to converse. I have never heard anyone go on and on about nothing the way she can. I know she's not your favorite person, Robin, but Ben's great, did you have a good time?" So very David to make plans for the evening and think only after it was over about my enjoyment.

"It was nice," I said, then added. "The restaurant was everything everyone has said." I knew this answer would make him happy.

"It was great. Perfect decor!" David continued to discuss all the fine points of the restaurant. I made the appropriate responses, but my mind was on my chickadee guest. Then my thoughts went to Joanne's dog. I knew I would give up Florida in a minute to have a little dog. Surprised at myself, I jumped.

"What's wrong?" David asked.

"Nothing, um, leg cramp. It's fine now, I loved the chandelier too." David continued his restaurant inventory. Would I give up Florida for a dog? I loved to travel. I realized I felt something missing in my life lately. Maybe I needed something to care for.

I glanced at David, who was still discussing the art in the restaurant's entrance. This reminded me of his response to Joanne's dog. I'll get some new plants this week.

"Robin, are you listening to me?"

"Huh? Of course, David."

"I said would you like to stop at the coffeehouse?"

"I'm really tired, David, is it alright if we just go home?"

"Sure. I hope you're not too tired, though," David said, as he squeezed my hand. I looked at David. He looked so handsome in his suit. I was so lucky. I squeezed his hand in return.

"No, I'm never too tired for you."

## Chapter 5

The sun shone through the French doors and lit up the entire living room. *There wouldn't be too many days left like this one,* I thought. I pulled my sweater tighter around me as I thought of the upcoming winter. I got ready to meet Jill for lunch. We had decided to meet at the cafe we like, across from Central Park. We thought we would make the most of this weather and sit in their garden room.

The previous day was still on my mind, as I put on my shoes. We had lounged around in bed most of the Sunday. We got up, one time, for a long Jacuzzi bath and then again to order pizza. I smiled to myself as I tied my shoes. I loved days like that. David and I became so close. Not just physically, but emotionally. I got to see a side of David that I sometimes forgot existed, not just the calm, cool businessman. Those days reminded me of the sweet, caring, sometimes actually confused man that I married. He always carried himself in such complete control that I forgot how vulnerable he could be.

I got up and headed for the door, still smiling about yesterday.

"Hi Bill."

"Good morning, Mrs. Pierson, shall I call you a cab?"

"No thanks, Bill, it's such a beautiful day, I'll walk." I waved good-bye and walked the ten blocks to Central Park. Many people were out taking advantage of the warm day. Some of the older gentleman walkers were already bundled up against the October air, hats protecting their balding heads, their overcoats covering suits. Mothers were out walking babies a few more times, before the cold kept them and their babies indoors. The mothers were dressed in just long sleeved shirts or light sweaters to best appreciate the weather. Not so daring with their little ones, their babies already sported heavier coats and hats with earflaps tied snuggly under chins. Some even had mittens, which I thought a little extreme. I felt completely comfortable with a short-sleeved shirt and light cashmere sweater.

I saw Jill waiting outside the cafe as I approached.

"Robin!" she called. We kissed hello.

"I have our table already picked out," Jill said. The hostess, who was in the process of seating a young couple, turned and Jill caught her eye. Jill pointed to the table she wanted and the hostess escorted us and gave us menus.

"Hello, ladies. Would you care for a drink?" the hostess asked.

"I'll have a Bloody Mary, how about you, Robin?"

"That sounds good, I'll have the same." The hostess smiled and gave us menus. "Your waiter is Paul. He'll bring those drinks right out to you." We thanked her and looked at our menus.

"The seafood quiche is fabulous here," Jill said.

"That sounds good. I had it once before and loved it." The waiter, Paul, came with our drinks and we both ordered the quiche.

"Now tell me about your dress for the anniversary party! It will be such a wonderful surprise for Celia. They are the sweetest couple," Jill said as the waiter left.

Jill's husband, Tyler, and Stuart had become close when Tyler registered his plant research firm with Stuart's bank. I stirred the celery in my drink.

"It's lovely, David helped me choose it," I said.

"It must be nice to have a husband with such exquisite taste," Jill replied, with a wistful sigh. "Tyler can barely pick out his own clothes, let alone mine."

"Don't pick on Tyler ," I said, laughing. "He may not have clothes taste, but at least he knows the difference between a gentian and a bellflower." Tyler was a botanist. He and I had the most wonderful conversations about plants.

"That would be important to you," Jill said. "Who else would care? You two are the only ones I know that feel it should be considered a national holiday when the orchids begin to bloom."

"Well, it should be. Do you know how delicate orchids are? It's an amazing miracle that we have such a flower in existence at all."

"I'll remember to light a candle for them at church this Sunday," Jill said with sarcasm. I laughed. Jill was funny, she always had me laughing when we were together.

"I know I've said this before," Jill began. "But I just can't get over how I married a man totally enthralled with anything green, and you married a man who insisted your fern cannot spend the night inside the house!" I had related the fern story to Jill last week. "And me with my love of clothes," Jill continued "with a man who doesn't even know if he's dressed half the time. Your husband not only dresses himself well, but helps you choose clothes too! It's definitely the height of irony, I will never be able to get over it." We both laughed at that.

"Maybe the fates felt we needed a balance," I said. "Would you want to see Tyler and I living out in the jungle somewhere, half-naked?" That picture in our heads made us both double up in hysterical laughter. I was wiping my tearing eyes when the waiter came with our lunch. He smiled at our mirth.

"Some people definitely know how to have a good time," he said. Jill held up her empty Bloody Mary glass.

"Bring us a couple more of these and let the good old times roll." The waiter laughed and went to get us fresh drinks.

After lunch, Jill and I walked in Central Park. I had asked for some extra crackers when we were at the restaurant to feed my birds, as I called them. Jill teased me as we walked over the hill.

"Will the birds call out to you personally when we get down the hill, Robin? I bet the birds will be confused to see a Robin here this time of year." I groaned.

"That joke has been done too many times before. You can't beat my father's standing joke. He says if he knew I'd take such an interest in being at one with my name he would have named me Goldie and became a millionaire." Jill laughed.

"That is funny. I bet he tells that one a lot."

"To anyone that will listen. David has heard it at least fifty times and to his credit, he still smiles when Dad tells it."

We were chatting when we passed the playground. There was the boy. I suddenly stopped. Jill stopped to see what I was looking at. There was no question, he was the same little boy. This time he was on the swings. He swung so high, his feet could almost touch the low branch of the tree planted nearby. He had on only a short-sleeved t-shirt and it looked like the same jeans as before. His lack of warm clothes made him stand out from the other warmly dressed children.

The elderly couple he seemed to be with were sitting on the same bench. The man was dozing again. The woman was reading a tabloid newspaper.

"Why are we stopping? I don't see any birds," Jill said.

"Do you see that boy on the swing?" I said, choking down the anger in my voice. Jill was surprised by my tone and stared at me.

"Yes, so?"

"Look how he's dressed. He must be freezing."

"He looks happy to me, Robin, he must be used to it."

"Used to it? Does that excuse not dressing him properly against this cold? Because he is used to it?"

"What are you getting so upset about?"

"I don't know," I answered, and really I didn't know. "Maybe I should say something to his grandparents, or whoever they are."

"What are you going to say? There's no crime in not putting a sweater on a kid."

"Oh, come on, Jill! Does he look well cared for?"

"Robin, what's with you? What's this kid to you?"

"I don't know ," I repeated helplessly.

"Robin, let's go ," Jill said, starting to walk away. "Your birds are waiting." I hesitated, shrugged my shoulders, and began walking. Jill was right. Who was he to me? I walked faster to catch up to Jill. I turned my head to take one last glance at him.

Jill and I sat down on my usual bench and immediately were surrounded by birds. Not many, most had left for warmer places. Jill and I chatted as we fed the birds. The light-heartedness I had felt at lunch was gone. Jill noticed this.

"What's wrong, Robin? You've gotten quieter since we left the playground. Does it have something to do with that boy?"

"Yes, no, I'm not sure."

"Okay, that's a definite answer, Robin."

"I saw that boy in the park last week, and for some reason, I can't put him out of my mind. Is that strange?"

"Maybe for some people, but not for you, our resident Mother Theresa."

"Jill, I'm serious."

"Did you say anything to David?"

"No, what can I say? I mean, that I saw a boy in the park that I think needs help and that I can't get him out of my head. He'd say to stop talking nonsense and spend less time at the park."

"Yep, he probably would say that. Why do you think he needs help?"

"I don't know. That's the problem. I'm not sure why he's stuck in my mind. You're right though. The boy did look happy on that swing. I think I just need a change of scenery. Did I tell you that David and I are going to Florida over the New Year?"

"No, that's great. Tyler and I are going on a cruise to the Caribbean."

"On how nice!"

"Why don't you go with us? Wouldn't it be fun to cruise together?"

"That would be great! David likes cruising, and he and Tyler get along well."

"Robin, David likes anyplace that he gets treated like a king."

"Jill!" I laughed, and playfully slapped her arm. As we discussed travel plans, I pushed the boy to the back of my mind again.

On the way home, I stopped at the nursery. It is a small place, sandwiched between a small delicatessen and a hardware store. The front is deceiving. You could never imagine plants being housed within. When you walked into the store, it widened and led to a huge greenhouse filled with an amazing assortment of plants.

"Hi, Steve. How are you on this beautiful day?" I said to my favorite plant person.

"Great, Mrs. Pierson, I ordered the day lilies for you. They should be here in a week. Day lilies were hard to find at this time of year. Why do you want them?"

"I wanted to see how they would thrive in my greenhouse in winter," I said, as I eyed some evening primroses.

"These primroses are lovely."

"Yeah, we just got them in," Steve replied.

I chose two primrose plants and also two more geraniums. "Can you send Mike out with these tomorrow before one o'clock?" Mike usually delivered my flowers.

"Sure, thing, do you want me to save the bill until the lilies come in?"

"Fine, Steve." I've been a regular customer of Steve's for three years. He knew I would probably buy something else before the lilies come in. I left Steve and headed out the door.

Outside, I decided to stop at the delicatessen and pick up dinner for David and I. This was another one of our places. I usually bring home dinner from the delicatessen at least twice a week.

"Hi, Sam, how's the knishes today?"

"Mrs. Pierson, darling! Are you ready to hit the road with me? We can get a little truck, maybe, sell corned beef from town to town." I laughed.

"Anytime, Sam, but what would David say if I were missing?"

"Oh, well, we'll take him too, he can be in charge of the pickles." Now I really laughed.

Sam smiled at me, showing a few of his missing teeth. He's a very sweet man, in his late seventies. He is rather stooped with sparse grey hair on top of his head, and a full grey beard and mustache. He has the greatest sense of humor, which he serves up liberally with every order.

"I don't think we can join you on the road, but I will take some of your corned beef."

"How much, darling?"

"Half a pound and half pound of pastrami. Also a couple of knishes, and a rye bread. Oh, and two cream sodas."

"There you go, sweetheart." Sam filled a bag with the order and threw in pickles and spicy mustard. I paid him, and blew him a kiss, which he pretended to catch.

I put the deli in the refrigerator and went into the bedroom to put away my sweater. I heard David come in as I came out of the room.

"Hi love," I said, as I wrapped my arms around him.

"I smell pickles, it must be pastrami night," he said as he kissed me.

"You guessed it ," I said.

"That means there should be a plant delivery tomorrow ," David said, as he took off his coat and walked into the bedroom.

"Ha, ha ," I called even though he was right. He walked back into the kitchen a minute later, already changed into casual clothes.

"You're not denying it," he said.

"So what if I'm not?"

He laughed and playfully smacked my bottom. "I'm not building any more greenhouses out there, so you better not fill this one up too fast."

"There's plenty of room," I said, and poured him some wine and handed him the glass. He took the glass and smiled.

"How was your day?" I asked.

"Great, the jewelry store account will be a go, I'm sure. Ben and I wined and dined them at lunch and they seemed pleased."

"With you and Ben, how could they not be pleased?"

"Hmm." That response earned me another longer kiss this time.

"And how's my gardener? Did you leave the plant world today at all?"

"Yes, I had lunch with Jill at that garden cafe across from Central Park."

"That nice. How's Jill doing?" David said, as he sifted through the mail.

"Great! Tyler and her are busy planning a trip to the Caribbean for over New Year's. Jill and I were talking about how much fun it would be if we all went together. Remember how much fun it was when we all went to the Cayman Islands last spring?"

"I remember you and Tyler going off on a lot of plant excursions. How are we going to be in Florida and the Caribbean at the same time?" he said smiling, as if he already knew the answer to that question. I hugged his arm and leaned against his shoulder.

"I wouldn't mind not going to Florida. And we both love to cruise."

"That's fine," he said hugging me with one arm, the other still holding his wine glass. "You girls make the arrangements."

"Oh, David, I love you. You are so good to me."

"Yes, I am, and don't you forget it."

I laughed and playfully pinched him as I went to put dinner on the table.

I snuggled on David's shoulder as we talked about the anniversary party in bed. We had just made love, and I was feeling warm and happy, and a little sleepy. David was saying how excited Stuart was.

"He is so sure that Celia is going to be completely surprised. I can't wait to see Celia's face when she walks into the party on Saturday night. She thinks she's going to a quiet anniversary dinner just for two. Did I tell you that her two sisters and their kids are flying in from Paris?"

"No, you didn't, David. You did tell me her brother was coming from Lyon." Celia grew up in Lyon. She met Stuart when she was on vacation here in New York, thirty-four years ago. They had a love at first sight relationship. Before they married, they wrote letters and called back and forth from Paris to New York two or three times a week. Stuart flew there often for weekends.

Stuart loves to talk about their courtship, as if it were a movie. When they married, Stuart had already taken over his father's banking business. Of course, he has built up the empire over the last thirty-five years that he's been president. It troubles him that Celia still has most of her family in Paris, even though she spends every June with them, except this past year when she was not well enough to travel.

Of course, having their two sons in the business with Stuart had helped.

"I can't wait to see the expression on Celia's face. Especially with all her family at the party," I said, as I snuggled closer to David. I think he made another comment on the party, but I was asleep before I could answer.

## Chapter 6

Tuesday morning came bright and clear. It was another beautiful day, but colder. I put on a-shirt and-jeans to work in the greenhouse. I wanted to rearrange some of the plants before my new ones arrived.

The door bell rang. It was Anne, my cleaning woman.

"Hi Anne, how are you today?"

"Just fine, Mrs. Pierson. You look like you're ready for the garden."

"Yes, I'm doing plant work. I expect some new plants to be delivered this morning. Also, a new dress will be delivered as well. Please listen for the buzzer, okay?"

"Sure thing, Mrs. Pierson, you might want to put on a sweater. It's pretty cold outside."

"Thanks, Anne." I grabbed a sweatshirt and put it on as I went out onto the patio. Soon, I was lost in my plant world.

"Your plants are here, Mrs. Pierson. Mike is bringing them out," Anne said, startling me out of my daydreams.

"Thanks, Anne," I said, as I stood up and brushed dirt off my-jeans.

"Hi, Mike, how are you?"

"Great, Mrs. Pierson, how ya doing?"

"Fine, thanks, here let me help you, Mike." I put the plants in the areas I had readied for them. Mike hauled in the two bags of soil I ordered. I walked Mike inside and tipped him.

"Thanks, Mrs. Pierson. Steve said he's ordered the lilies and they'll be in sometime next week. Steve will call you when they're in."

"Okay, tell him to send me the bill."

"I'll just bring it when we deliver the lilies."

"Great. See you then, Mike."

As I was showing Mike out, the buzzer rang.

"Yes, Bill?"

"Dress delivery for you, Mrs. Pierson."

"Thanks, Bill. Send him up."

I went into the bedroom with the dress. Anne was in there dusting.

"What do you think, Anne?"

"Wow! It's beautiful! Is that for the anniversary party?" I had told Anne about the party the week before.

"Yes, David picked it out."

"Mr. Pierson! Gosh, he has great taste."

"Yes, he does." I walked into the closet and hung it up. I went into the bathroom and changed my t-shirt and sweatshirt. When I came out, Anne was dusting the study.

"I'm going to the park for a while, Anne."

"It's getting pretty cold for the park," Anne replied.

"I know. I've been going almost every day. I want to feed the birds before they all fly south. I feel like I'm starting them off with a good meal before their long journey." Anne laughed.

"Do you want me to make dinner tonight?" On the days Anne cleaned, I sometimes had her do a little cooking for me when I didn't want to be bothered with making dinner. I looked at my watch, two-thirty.

"Yeah, that would be great. I have the ingredients for lasagna, you can make that."

"No problem, have fun at the park."


Bill hailed a cab for me. I was tired from the garden work and the cold didn't help. Autumn is such an interesting time of year. One day can be so warm, and the next freezing. I hopped out at the park entrance. After paying the cabbie, I took a moment to make sure I took that extra bag of bread. It was there along with my crackers, and I even had some croutons. I wanted to make sure my birds were well cared for.

I walked taking my usual detour through the playground. There were only a few children today. Two little girls, well bundled up, were playing in the sandbox. I watched them for a moment as they made sand pies. One girl got up to give some to her mother. The mother smiled at her, exclaimed over her creation, and took a pretend bite. Then she gave the pie to the woman she was talking to, who also pretended to take a nibble.

After a few words of praise, the little girl went back to join her friend, her expression on her face showing definite satisfaction with her baking skills.

I smiled and looked at the monkey bars. At the bench behind the bars sat the same elderly couple. This time, they were both sleeping. The man snored and the women groaned. I looked around for the little boy and couldn't see him. My first reaction was worry. I stopped and argued with myself. *Are you insane, Robin?* I thought. *You don't even know this kid. Why are you wondering where he is? He's probably not even here. He's probably at a friend's house or a relative or whatever, it's none of my concern.* I gave myself a little shake and marched off to my bench.

As I rounded the corner and walked toward my bench, a smile came to my face as I saw my birds clustered about. It was almost as if they knew what time I would arrive. Then I froze and the smile froze too. There he was! The little boy from the playground was sitting on my bench. He was smiling and whistling (or I guess as close as he could get to whistling). He was still wearing only a T-shirt, streaked with dirt, and the same jeans. Maybe his jeans just all looked the same, dirty and with holes. I walked to the bench, almost feeling as if I was intruding on his conversation with the birds.

The boy stopped whistling. He looked up at me, smiled and displayed perfect baby teeth in his dirt-smudged face. His dirty blond hair fell across his face. His lovely large hazel eyes still stared at me. He watched me, friendly, but wary. He was ready to retreat if he had to. He had a cute button nose, centered between rosy cheeks, or actually very cold cheeks. I then noticed a shiver that seemed to go through his entire body. I slowly approached him and sat at the edge of the bench away from him.

"Are you cold?" I asked.

"Yea," he admitted. I pulled off my sweatshirt and tossed it to him. It landed on his lap. He picked it up and looked at me, questioning.

"Put it on, it's okay. I have a sweater in my back pack," I said, as I rummaged through my pack. I pulled out a sweater and put it on. I looked at the little boy. He was trying to figure out how to wear the sweatshirt.

"Let me help you," I said, as I took the sweatshirt and pulled it over his head. I helped him pull his arms through and rolled up the sleeves. He hugged his arms together and gave me a big smile, just showing a hint of a dimple. I smiled back.

"What's your name?" I asked.

"Max, what yours?"

"Robin." Max went back to hugging his arms and trying to whistle at the birds.

"Do you want to feed the birds, Max? I have some crackers and bread." He slowly reached for some bread. He watched me as I tore off pieces and threw them to the birds. Max laughed as he followed my lead, and the birds pushed and shoved each other for the bread.

"Those birds are sure hungry," Max said.

"Yes, they are. I'm hungry too," I said as I ate a cracker. "Would you like a cracker?" He hesitated just a second. Then cautiously reached for a few crackers. He ate them quickly and I gave him some more.

"You're just like the birds," I said. He laughed at that. We sat quietly for a few minutes while we tossed the bread and crackers to the birds. Max continued to laugh now and then at their antics.

"Max! Where the hell are you?" Max and I both jumped as the woman's scream seemed to echo around us. It disturbed our peaceful serenity like a rock thrown into a still pond.

"Max!" Now a man's loud bellow followed. "You better get the hell over here, boy!" Max jumped up, and almost frantically began pulling off the sweatshirt. I reached to help him. When it was off, he quickly ran toward the playground. He stopped at the top of the hill and turned to look at me, yelled, "Bye," and took off.

I sat frozen to the bench. Should I go after him? I got up and jogged to the corner. I saw Max reach the older couple. The old man grabbed his arm and yelled something I couldn't hear.

Then the old man let him go and turned to go with the old woman. Max trailed behind them, kicking at a rock in his way. The old man turned around and said something. Max jogged up, until he was right behind them, as they made their way to the entrance.

I slowly turned back to my bench. I walked over and mechanically sat down. I felt exhausted. I could barely move. Almost as if I had gone through some ordeal. Mindlessly, I took out the croutons and tossed them to the birds. I watched as they ate. What had happened here? I tried to sort it all out. I met a little boy who helped me feed the birds. That was all. Then why did I feel so distraught? Yes his, grandparents or whatever they are seemed to be a nasty sort, but I see that kind every day. I told myself to let it go.

This rational train of thought seemed to help. I finished tossing the croutons to the birds and got up to leave. I picked up the sweatshirt to stuff it in the bag. I caught a whiff of a new scent. A mixture of dirt and sweat. Something else too, not a male scent, but a little boy. The scent of Max. I stuffed the shirt into the back pack and swung it over my shoulder as I walked to the park's entrance. I walked home hoping it would help clear my thoughts.


I had just emerged from the bedroom when David came in. He walked to the kitchen and threw the mail on the counter.

"Greetings from Maui from your parents," David said as he held up a postcard. "They must be back in Connecticut by now. This postmark is from last week." Both sets of parents still lived in Connecticut.

"What does the card say?" I asked. He handed me the postcard,

"The usual, wish you were here, and so on, and so forth," David replied as he went to the refrigerator for some wine.

"Lasagna! Great!" he said as he took the wine bottle out.

"Compliment of Anne," I said.

"She makes the best, well maybe second best, after all, there is yours."

"Thanks," I said as I went to hug him. "How was your day?" I asked.

"The usual. All talk is devoted to the anniversary party and all that pertains to it."

"My dress came today," I interrupted. "I can't wait to wear it. It's so lovely."

"What did you do today, Robbie?" David asked as he kissed me.

"I spent the morning waiting for deliveries. My plants came today, too."

"Is there still room to move in the greenhouse or have the plants taken over?"

"There is still plenty of room, thank you very much, sir," I said smartly. David went into the bedroom, calling over his shoulder,

"So you spent the day at home?" I hesitated, before I answered. Should I mention my encounter with Max? I bit my lip and decided to cautiously go ahead.

"No, I went to the park to feed the birds."

"You did?" he said absently.

"Yes, there aren't many left, most have flown south."

"It was chilly today, did you take a sweater?"

"Yes I did." David came back out of the bedroom, and gave me a smile as he pulled on a sweater over his head.

"Good."

I put the lasagna in the oven. David went to light a fire in the fireplace.

"I met a little boy at the park," I said to the back of David's head. He was concentrating on putting the right amount of newspaper into the fireplace to get the fire started.

"Did you?" he again said absently.

"Yes, he was sitting on the bench where I usually feed the birds. I gave him some bread and we fed the birds together."

"That's nice," David said, not giving this conversation any real attention. I could understand why. It didn't sound that interesting to my ears either. I had no idea what point I was trying to make. I continued to rattle on.

"He was sweet, rather dirty though. I wasn't sure who was caring for him. He was with an older couple. They didn't seem too responsible." David had the fire going by now. He sat back on his heels, and stared into the flames. When I spoke of the condition of Max and the older couple, he turned around and looked at me. I knew that look. It was the 'just before anger' look. He spoke softly, but sternly.

"Why are you telling me this, Robin? And what the hell does it have to do with you?" His eyes narrowed, and turned emerald green. They looked twins to mine, yet his eyes made me flinch. I knew how angry he was becoming. I stopped setting the table and looked at the floor.

"It has nothing to do with me, David. I'm just telling you about what happened at the park."

"And that's all?" he asked, still stern, eyes still green.

"That's all," I said. He turned back to the fire and sighed.

"Good, as long as these encounters stay at the park."

"Of course, David. Come, dinner is ready."


"Did you make the arrangements for the cruise today?" David asked as I cleaned the dinner plates and put them in the dish washer.

"I'll call Jill tomorrow. There's plenty of time."

"Those winter cruises fill up fast. Make sure we get a suite on the outside. I like to see where the boat's going."

"I will, David. I'll make the arrangements tomorrow," I repeated, feeling guilty and not knowing why. I finished the dishes and sat down beside David on the sofa. He read the Wall Street Journal and sipped brandy. His usual after dinner routine. I snuggled up to him. He tried to keep on reading. He pretended to ignore me, but I saw the smile on his lips slowly grow. I began kissing his shoulder, then his neck.

"Hey, watch the brandy!" he exclaimed.

"Why? Is it going to do a trick?" I replied, laughing. David put down the brandy and grabbed me.

"I'll show you a trick," he growled and bit into my neck. I squealed, and we rolled off the sofa.

## Chapter 7

The rest of the week was filled with last minute shopping for the party. On Saturday, I took time to have a manicure, pedicure, and have my hair done. Jill, with my input, made travel plans and booked a fun-filled week to the Caribbean for Mid-January. We had originally planned to go over Christmas and New Year, but both of my brothers were going to their spouse's families, and I didn't want my parents to be alone over Christmas. Jill and I booked adjoining cabin suites, and we were already into discussing our shopping expedition for a new wardrobe fit for the high seas.

I didn't go back to the park. The encounter with Max wasn't mentioned again. It seemed as if the whole meeting happened in a dream. I realized that it was real though, and thoughts of Max trailed through my mind throughout the week.

David had coordinated his ensemble by the time I emerged from the shower. I pulled my shower cap off carefully, to protect Antonio's hair design. As I watched, David put on his tuxedo. I reminded myself how handsome he was and how lucky I was to have him.

I turned back to the powder room to do my makeup. Face finished. David had already finished dressing and was putting on gold cuff-links, when I walked to the closet. I pulled on stockings and a long body slip, and then carefully stepped into the gown. David zipped my gown, and helped me on with my diamond necklace and matching earrings. He gently turned me around. His eyes showed his pleasure.

"You are stunning," He said.

"We do make a handsome pair, I'll have to watch you around the ladies tonight," I laughed.

"Don't worry, I'll be too busy keeping the men away from you to pay attention to the ladies." I laughed again and hugged his arm. David picked up my heavy wrap, and stared at it with displeasure.

"You need a fur," he said. "I'm not going to take no for an answer this time."

"No way, we've had this discussion before and I won't budge on this issue. I won't wear a dead animal. Do you know how many minks it takes to make just one coat?" I said.

"Yes. You've told me enough times ," he said, as he put my wrap on.

"Well, then stop asking me to get one and I'll stop telling you."

"Alright, alright, I'll stop asking. Sometimes I worry about your head, Robin." Shaking his own head, he went out the door. I picked up the purse that I had dyed to match my dress and shoes and followed right behind.

We arrived at the hotel just a few minutes before eight o'clock. Celia was expected about eight-thirty. Stuart wanted all his guests there by eight. Stuart didn't want to take the chance of Celia bumping into anyone she knew in the lobby. We had the valet park our car, and took the elevator up to the top floor. Cocktails and hors d'oeuvres were being served, as the band played.

What a view. The walls were made of glass and you could see Manhattan at its most beautiful; at night. I went to the powder room, checked my hair and put on my party smile. When I came out, I saw David talking to Douglas. Douglas is Stuart's son. Douglas was excited, and extremely nervous. I went over and kissed his cheek.

"Robin, I almost didn't recognize you. At first glance, I thought we were being honored by having a visiting princess attend our humble party." I laughed.

"Thank you Douglas, but I don't think I would use the word humble to describe this party."

"Oh? And what word would you use?" he enquired.

"Magnificent," I said.

"I hope my mom thinks so ," Douglas replied, smiling at my compliment.

"Celia will be enchanted. You guys outdid yourselves ," David added.

"Thank you both. If you will excuse me, I must check on some last minute details."

Douglas left us, just as we spotted Jill and Tyler. Jill looked lovely, which I exclaimed as I kissed her cheek. She wore a black, strapless gown that flowed beautifully down to the floor. Around her neck she wore the diamonds that Tyler had given her on their fifth anniversary. She had also had her hair done. It was pulled up with curls hanging down her neck.

The men left to get drinks.

"This is a stunning place for a party," Jill remarked. It was true. The chandeliers, which hung down from the ceiling, shined brightly, their crystal prisms hanging low. The walls were a soft teal. Fresh flowers held in baskets lined the walls. The tables held huge bouquets of white and pink roses, on creamy white tablecloths. There was a large wooden dance floor where many couples danced.

"The designer Stuart hired did an excellent job," I replied.

"Oh, by the way, Robin, I spoke to the travel agent today. She confirmed the cruise. We are set for Mid-January and we did get the outside suites."

"Good," I replied. "I can't wait, we'll have such a good time."

"What are you girls discussing with such beaming smiles?" Tyler asked as the men came over with our drinks.

"Cruise talk. We are all set for Mid- January," Jill answered.

"Lying on the deck, drinking Margaritas, now that's my idea of a vacation!" Tyler said.

"Sounds wonderful. We haven't been to the Caribbean since we've were dating, right, Robbie?" David added.

"True. What a nice trip that was. We stayed in a little resort in St. Lucie, right on the beach. We took long walks on the beach at night and swam in the lagoon while the sun rose. It was so romantic."

"Ah, the dating days. When every day is filled with adventure, how exciting those days were," Jill said.

"You mean exhausting. I get tired just thinking about them," David said, as he and Tyler both laughed. Jill and I just gave each other exasperated looks. Jill was about to reply when Douglas called out.

"They're coming!" The band stopped playing, lights were turned off, and everyone got quiet. We heard Celia at the doorway.

"Stuart, are we having dinner up here? Oh good, I love the view," Celia exclaimed as she stepped through the door and Stuart turned on the lights.

"Surprise!" everyone yelled at once. Celia looked stunned. Then, she smiled and reached for Stuart. Everyone applauded as they hugged and kissed and walked down the entrance stairs. Celia stopped every second to hug someone else. Jill and I wiped away tears. David put his arm around my shoulder and squeezed me tight.

Stuart led Celia up to the dance floor. Celia looked lovely in a long burgundy evening gown. She was still a little too thin from her illness, but that seemed to be the only lasting effect. Stuart kept his arm around Celia, love shining in his eyes as he looked at her. Tears flowed out of mine.

"That was a great party," David said as he undressed. He carefully smoothed his bowtie and put it on top of his tuxedo, already hung on the hanger ready to go to the cleaners tomorrow. I slipped out of my dress and hung it next to the tuxedo. I stretched my arms wide as I yawned.

"It was lovely," I replied." I think I have never seen Celia so surprised or so happy." David smiled as he caught my arms as I was lowered them down in midair. He placed them around his neck and looked at me with a quirky grin.

"A penny for your thoughts," I whispered. David kissed my cheek and then my neck.

"I want to be them in thirty years. I want you to always look at me the way Celia looked at Stuart as she walked through the door."

It was so rare that David expressed his innermost feelings, that I was caught off guard. I made my reply light to offset his intensity. "I think that it's possible, especially it you rent out the top floor of the hotel for our anniversary party." David grinned as he lifted me and carried me up to the bed.

"I was thinking of maybe booking Buckingham Palace, if that's alright with you," he said, as he laid me across the bed and carefully lay down on top of me.

"I don't know, I'd have to deal with all that royalty, but I guess it will do." Then I added wickedly. "But, only if you promise me you'll not invite Joanne." David laughed loudly and pinched my bottom." She'll probably be too busy bragging over Bitsy's great-granddogs. We can't expect the sweet little things to travel in a crate overseas, now can we?" David mimicked in a squeaky imitation of Joanne. It was my turn to laugh as I rolled on top of him.

"What's your pleasure, sir?" I asked, my eyes gleaming. David smiled wickedly as his eyes raked me from head to toe.

"Oh, the things a girl needs to do to get to England nowadays," I said laughing. David growled savagely and rolled me on top of him.

## Chapter 8

David announced, "Monday has come too soon!" The feelings of well-being spilled over to Sunday from the party. We had spent most of Sunday in bed full of contentment with just being together.

After David left for work on Monday, I went to work in the greenhouse. It was a cold October morning. I sighed as I realized in a couple of months, I'd think of this as a warm morning. My thoughts were about what David said to me as we lounged in bed Sunday. He talked about future trips we should take together. He wanted to get back to Paris, maybe this summer, and spend some time in the wine country.

That would have sounded like castles in the air from anyone else, but not David. He was already, in his mind, making a decision on when to see the travel agent to book dates.

I paused in my thoughts as I added soil to one of my geraniums. I looked at the buildings across the way. I could just see the top of the hotel where Celia's party was. My mind went over the party, not the decor or the music, but the way Celia danced with her sons. The way Celia held onto her son's hands when she thanked everyone for being there to celebrate this great moment in her life. Douglas, the older son, had kissed her cheek when she finished and Celia caressed his hair. *What joy children bring,* I thought. As much as Celia loved Stuart, the way she looked at her sons filled me with a feeling of warmth that I had never experienced before. I bet Douglas was an adorable little boy with those big brown eyes and sandy blond hair. I could imagine Celia tucking him in at night, reading him stories. I could see Stuart playing baseball with him and teaching him how to ice skate at Rockefeller Center. I sat back on my heels, my spade held absently in my hand as I gazed up at the cloudless sky.

I gave myself a little shake and stabbed the dirt viciously with the spade. What was I thinking? Even after four years of marriage, I knew David was not ready for children any more than I was. We both loved to travel and we both valued our freedom. There was no room in our life for children. These thoughts jumbled in my head, but I wondered whose thoughts they were, mine or David's. I continued to stab my spade into the dirt, trying to settle my thoughts. In my confusion , I accidentally cut off a flower head from my marigold. .

"Oh sweetie, I'm sorry!" I said to the decapitated marigold head. I put down my spade and took a deep breath. *I'd better leave here before I have no plants left,* I thought ruefully.

I walked inside and changed my shirt. I put on a clean sweatshirt and decided to walk to the park. I thought the walk might calm me, maybe, I added, some of my birds were still here.

The park was quiet. Only a few children played at the playground. Then I saw the elderly couple who watched Max. I scanned the playground, but didn't see Max. I walked over the hill quickly, and there he was on the same bench. He sat quietly, swinging his legs. The thought hit me suddenly, *Did he wait for me every time he was there?* I felt almost guilty for not being at the park daily. *That's ridiculous,* I thought. I have no obligations to rearrange my life around meeting Max in the park. What have I gotten myself into? I felt angry at Max for making me feel this way. I walked to the bench, trying not to let my emotions show on my face.

"Hi, Robin!" Max said, excitedly. I couldn't believe he remembered my name. The anger melted from me as quick as it came.

"Hi, Max. Are you supposed to be here?" I didn't want a repeat of last time.

"It's okay. I can hear Ms. Johnson from here." Ms. Johnson? I guessed they were not Max's grandparents. Maybe the babysitter?

"Max, does Ms. Johnson take care of you all day?"

"Yeah, night too." So, he lived with them. The mystery thickened.

"You bring bread, Robin?" I smiled and held out the bag. I guess that was enough information for now, even though my curiosity was peaked. Max and I threw bread at the few birds until we heard the familiar yell. Max jumped up and was about to run off. I impulsively bent over and gave him a quick hug. He looked at me strangely and then smiled before he left.

I watched him run over the hill, thinking how cold his arms were in that thin shirt.

After David and I made love that night, I stared at the ceiling. I listened to David's breathing. The park had only made me feel more unsettled than before. Thankfully, David didn't notice my preoccupation. I didn't even want to attempt to explain how I was feeling. I really didn't know myself. I decided not to visit the park.

# Chapter 9

"I sure hope this weather clears up," Celia said, looking out the window. The wind thrashed the trees relentlessly. Celia sighed and turned back to the goodie bags she was filling.

"All this work! Such a disappointment to the children if all this blows away."

"It's early yet, Celia," I said, as I counted bat and ghost cookies that I put into boxes. "The wind will die down, by four."

Only three days ago, Celia was so happy at the women's league. She had made a speech that inspired us all.

"I am so pleased with all the hard work everyone has put in these last weeks. I think this is going to be one of our best fundraisers!" Celia had announced. Everyone clapped. It was the last formal meeting of our women's league before the Halloween festival. It was Celia's idea to have the party at Central Park, and to make it more of a party than a fundraiser.

After the children's party, we were having a huge auction to benefit the women's shelter. As Celia spoke, I could still see a glow of happiness from the anniversary party. We had lunch the week before and the party was all we had talked about. She told me about the fun she had with her relatives after the party. Her sister had just flown back to Paris the day before we met for lunch. I was happy for her. I think it gave her extra energy for this fundraiser. I hadn't seen her display such exuberance in a long time.

Now though, her face was grim with concern.

Celia remained nervous despite my continuous reassurances. We had been at Celia's apartment since ten that morning getting last minute preparations ready.

Celia's penthouse overlooked Central Park, I walked over to the window to look out. The fall leaves were all over the ground and hills.

"Do you think we will be able to set up the stage for the auction? I knew we should have rented a hall for this event," Celia said, angry at herself. This auction was to be the big money maker for the shelter. Stuart himself donated two brand new computers for the event. Celia, myself, and the rest of the women's club spent months getting businesses to donate to the auction. We did very well. The auction would have items ranging from televisions, to gift certificates, to Broadway shows and dinners at Manhattan's trendiest restaurants.

As president of the women's club, Celia took on the bulk of responsibility for the outcome of the event.

"Celia, we all voted that your idea to have it in Central Park was wonderful. It's a lovely setting for a Halloween festival. Remember, we felt we would limit our attendance if we didn't have it at a central location. Besides, the stage is extremely sturdy at Central Park, and there's a cover to pull around the outside if the weather gets too horrible. Don't be gloomy. The weatherman on NBC said we would have clear skies tonight and it will be a lovely, but brisk evening with the temperature hovering at sixty-three degrees. I did my best weatherman imitation and Celia laughed.

"Robin, you are always a ray of sunshine."

"Are the Banfords back from Portugal yet?" I asked.

"Oh, yes, they'll be there tonight and you'll never guess what Edith brought back!".

We chatted and took a short break for lunch. After lunch, more of the women's club members came to help us organize last minute things. The things for the auction were being taken by a moving company we hired, and some of the movers were getting the last minute things taken over.

Thankfully, the weatherman was true to his word. The wind stopped and the sun shone. I got into my costume. I decided to dress up as part of the spirit of the occasion. I dressed all in black, from thick black leggings, to a long heavy black dress. I had a long black wig and a pointy black hat with a crescent moon embroidered on its front. I painted a tiny black star on my cheek and made my lips a dark red. After I grabbed my wand, I joined Celia. She had dressed like Mother Goose and was adorable. Most of us decided to show the Halloween spirit by dressing for the occasion. We exclaimed over each other before leaving for the park at two-thirty.

At four o'clock we were ready. We had set all the game booths toward the left of the playground area, and children were already coming to see what we had. I was in charge of tickets for the games. We only charged a quarter a ticket so that everyone was able to join in the fun. There was a haunted house with minor scares, food and snacks galore, and at five o'clock, a costume contest for the kids. The prize was a gift certificate to a toy store. There were also goodie bags filled with treats for children to leave with.

I watched as the costumed children came over to get tickets. They were so cute, and so many. I lost count of all the super heroes and animal costumes. The children's mothers exclaimed over the decorations, and thanked us for putting on such a wonderful event. I felt very proud and happy to be a part of it all. This was my favorite part of the festival, even though I knew Celia looked forward to six-thirty when the auction would begin.

Stuart and his sons would help run the auction. David promised he would be there by six o'clock to lend a hand. I watched the children play games, when I heard a small voice say, "Can I play too?"

I turned around and smiled, it was Max. My smile froze on my face. I looked at Max in astonishment. He wasn't dressed in a costume, only the same jeans and worn sneakers. At least he had on a sweatshirt, though it looked too small for him.

"Hi Max." Max just looked at me. I forgot I was in costume. "It's me, Robin, I bring the bread for the birds." Max looked a while longer then recognition dawned on his face and he smiled.

"What ya doin all dressed funny like that?" I realized then he had no idea why anyone was in costume, and probably was wondering what was going on at the park.

"It's Halloween, sweetheart." Still no bells went off. "It's a day, Max, when kids and adults dress up in funny costumes and play games and things." I wasn't sure if he understood me. He looked confused, then sad.

"I don't have any costume. Can I play games?" He looked at me with eyes only too used to disappointment. I said nothing. He started to leave, his hand wiping a quick tear away. I shook myself from out of my trance and reached for his small, dirty hand.

"Of course you can play, Max!" I looked quickly around for his guardians. They sat on a bench. They were talking with another older couple. I told one of my helpers that I would be back. I grabbed a bunch of tickets and walked with Max toward the games.

Max played bean bag toss and ring toss. I got him popcorn and cookies. I overheard a couple of inquisitive children asking why that boy wasn't wearing a costume. Max didn't seem to hear, or he was having too much fun to let it bother him.

I kept glancing back to see if his guardians noticed he was not on the playground. They were still engrossed in their conversation. I took Max into the haunted house. He yelled back at the ghost that tried to scare him. Max pulled me along, whenever I stopped, unsure where to go next.

An hour had gone by since Max stumbled into me at the ticket table. Families were going home as twilight fell to darkness.

I grabbed one of the few goodie bags left and walked Max over to the foursome at the bench. They stopped their conversation and looked at me with a 'who the hell are you' expression. The woman who was always with Max at the park saw Max standing somewhat behind me.

"Max, what are you doing? Sorry, lady. Was he bothering you? Max, why you running off and bothering people! I've told ya to leave people alone!" Max was looking at his sneakers throughout this speech, and I hastened to interrupt her.

"Oh no, it's okay," I said. "I was working at the Halloween party. I saw your little boy and just wondered if he could have a Halloween goodie bag? Actually, I've seen Max play at the park other times I've been here. He looks to be such a sweet little boy, is he your grandson?" I didn't want to sound too nosy. I was pretty positive that he wasn't, but I needed to know Max's relationship with these people.

"No, he sure ain't that," the man said, glaring at his wife. "We already raised our own."

"Our name's Johnson," said the woman. "Max, here, is a foster child. Appreciate you letting him play your games."

"My pleasure. My name is Robin, Robin Pierson." I handed Mrs. Johnson the goody bag. Max's hands were full of trinkets he won at the games. Max smiled shyly at me. Mrs. Johnson heaved herself off the bench, along with the rest of the group.

"Well, I guess it's time to go home and fix some dinner. Come along, Max." Without another word they turned and left. Max trailed behind, turned, and waved to me one last time. Then, he jogged to catch up, clutching his trinkets. The mystery was solved. I knew about Max. Foster parents. I wasn't sure if that made the situation better or worse.

I turned and went to see if David had arrived yet.

David stood by the auction stage talking to Stuart. People filled the benches as they waited for the auction to begin. I crept behind David and then jumped out and yelled "Boo!" David turned toward me, looked me up and down with a 'you've got to be kidding' look and turned back to Stuart and resumed his conversation. Stuart laughed, David smiled, and I scowled and hit David on the shoulder.

"What no spell? I thought at least you could come up with an incantation to turn me into a frog or something ," David said, smirking.

"I wouldn't dream of insulting the amphibian world by adding you to them," I said glibly. David lunged for me, as Stuart doubled over laughing. I ran toward Celia.

"You'll pay for that one, Robin," David called after me, but I could tell by his smile that he wasn't really angry.

Celia spoke with the workers, who were placing the large auction items on the stage.

"How did the children's activities go?" she asked.

"Great! All the kids seemed to have a wonderful time."

"Good! Who was that little boy I saw you walking with?" I froze for a moment, I didn't think that anyone had noticed. What if Celia told Stuart? *What's the difference?* I asked myself, but then David might find out. Was

I hiding Max from David? All these thoughts and questions went through my head as Celia stared at me.

"I didn't mean to pry, Robin."

"Oh, no Celia, I'm sorry. The question just startled me. I didn't think anyone saw me with the boy. Not that there's anything wrong with me being with him." I babbled on trying to make some sense of what I was saying. Celia was about to comment when one of the workers asked her a question. She gave me one last look of concern.

"Let's talk later," she said, as she went to the worker. *What's wrong with me?* I asked myself. *Why does it bother me to talk about Max?*

"Robin!" David called for me to come sit near him. I pasted a smile on my face, and walked over to David.

The auction was a success. It brought in over 20,000 dollars for the women's shelter. Celia was radiant when she gave the check to the director of the shelter. Next, Celia would be off heading the fundraiser for the children's hospital. She is wonderful. Celia and I never did talk about Max. I think she forgot, and I didn't want to remind her. Besides what was there to talk about, anyway?

# Chapter 10

November flew by with incredible speed. I helped Celia with the hospital fundraiser, and looked forward to the Caribbean cruise. It was colder each day. I thought about Max. David had forgotten the kid at the park. I didn't know why my thoughts kept drifting back to him. I wondered what he was doing and if he were safe. I tried to get back to the park one day, early in the month, but it rained. I thought, hopefully, that even the Johnsons couldn't be out on a day like this. My days were caught up in fundraiser obligations. Still, I told myself, next week I'd get to the park.

Thanksgiving was a cold, crisp November day. Snow was expected. I could feel the temperature drop. I snuggled closer to David as we drove to his parents' house for dinner. Then later we would go to my parents to spend the night.

We have this alternating plan between parents for the past four years, it has worked well. David looked forward to seeing his younger brother, Justin, and his family.

Justin was an anthropologist. He had been in Egypt for the last two years, sponsored by the history museum. Now he was back to resume his position as director of the museum. His wife, Alaina, was pregnant with their third child. Their twins, Kayla and Kenneth, had just turned three.

We flew out to Egypt to see them the winter before and spent two weeks touring. I even accompanied Justin on one of his digs, which was exciting. David, of course, was more interested in learning about their banking system. It was amazing how different these two brothers were, I thought they got along so well because they were so different. Besides, Justin was the only sibling David had. I sighed inwardly. I wished I got along as well with my brothers.

I was a change of life baby. My brothers, Brandon and Ethan, were eight and ten years older than me. Brandon went to boarding school when

I turned five. Ethan left two years later. Except for holidays, I barely saw them. Moreover, when I did, I was the baby and usually treated as such.

Both my brothers are physicians in hospitals, one in California and one in Chicago. David and I have flown out a few times to visit. It was nice seeing my nieces and nephews, but I never feel the closeness that David feels for Justin.

"We'll be there in about ten minutes," David said. "Don't fall asleep, Robin." David glanced at me staring out the window. I turned to him and smiled.

"I'm daydreaming," I said. "I can't wait to see the twins. I bet they've grown."

"I think you bought them enough welcome home gifts," David said, ruefully, I laughed.

"It was fun shopping for little kid toys. My brother's kids are too old. All they want is money." I turned and looked at the wrapped presents covering the back seat. There were so many cute toys and clothes to choose from, I kept finding more and more things I liked.

My thoughts turned to Max and I frowned. I quickly looked back out the window so David wouldn't see my face. I felt a lump in my throat and a tightness in my chest as I remembered Max's face when he saw all the kids dressed up at Halloween. He looked so lost and overwhelmed. I wondered what he was doing today. I convinced myself that surely Mr. and Mrs. Johnson would have some kind of special dinner for Thanksgiving.

Justin and Alaina had just arrived as we pulled into his parents' driveway. I said a quick prayer for Max, and put thoughts of him away for the day.

Justin came over to us and David reached his hand out to shake Justin's.

"Sorry, mon frere, a handshake won't do after not seeing you for eleven months." He pulled David's hand into him and gave him a bear hug, slapping him on the back. I laughed and David blushed. David glared at me and I covered my mouth with my hand. David would never have stood for this from anyone else. He had resigned himself to Justin's exuberant nature long ago.

David took after his more standoffish father. David disentangled himself from Justin's grasp and prepared himself for his mother's affectionate hello, which was still to come. Justin came over to me and I hugged him hard.

"How's the most beautiful sister-in-law in the world? Remember, you can always come live with Alaina and me if my older brother isn't treating you like the princess you are. Right, Alaina?" I laughed and David glared at Justin. Poor David loved Justin, but couldn't keep up with his speedy repartee.

"Yes, yes Justin," Alaina answered, "But I think Robin has it pretty good where she is." David smiled at Alaina and kissed her cheek in welcome. She was used to Justin's teasing. Alaina knew she had nothing to fear. Justin worshiped the ground she walked on. I hugged and kissed Alaina in hello. She has always been my favorite sister-in-law.

"You look well, Alaina. How do you feel?"

"Well I'm not nauseous anymore, that's an improvement," she said, smiling.

"I've heard the second trimester is the most comfortable. Are you feeling flutters?"

"Just a few bubbles."

"There's Grammy's angels!" Alaina and I looked up to see Justin's and David's mother, Suzanne, reach for Kayla. Kenneth hung on to Justin's leg. Suzanne bent down and hugged them both. She whispered into their ears, which made them giggle. Suzanne stood up and hugged Justin then David. Alaina and I walked over to everyone.

"Alaina, dear!" Suzanne exclaimed "You look wonderful, positively glowing. I do believe you're beginning to show a bit."

"Not yet, I hope, Suzanne, I still have some months to go," Alaina replied.

"Well, you look radiant." Suzanne hugged Alaina and then me. Her eyes checked my slender body and I braced myself for what was coming next.

"Nothing yet, darling? Well, I'm sure soon, right, David?"

"I would think you have enough grandchildren. My brother is keeping you in a steady supply." At this, Justin punched David on the shoulder. David smiled and got into his boxer stance.

"None of that!" Suzanne said. "Honestly, when you boys are home, you act like teenagers again. Come, let's go see your father. He can't wait to show off the new Chagall he bought at the museum auction." Suzanne laced an arm through each of her sons and walked toward the house. Alaina and I each picked up one of the twins from the driveway where they were busily piling rocks, and followed.

"David fielded that question nicely," Alaina said.

"Yes," I replied grimly. "Do you think there will come a day when Suzanne stops asking that question at each visit?"

"Sure there will." Alaina replied smirking. "The day you show up pregnant." We both laughed and walked into the house.

Alaina knew it was David who was not interested in kids. David had no intention of letting his parents know his feelings. He let them think whatever they liked, and sidestepped any comments that came his way. Of course, that left me with some side-stepping to do myself. All of this left Suzanne with the impression that there was something lacking in me. Usually, once in every visit, I had to hear about some specialist I could see.

Marie, the housekeeper, helped us unbundle the twins and took all the coats upstairs. We followed everyone into the living room where the Chagall was hanging over the fireplace. Miles came over to Alaina and me, and kissed us both on the cheek. He went over to the twins who were looking at picture books on the sofa.

"How are my little Egyptians?" Miles always called them that even though they were born in New York. Alaina laughed. She sat on the sofa, and recounted the twins' newest accomplishments. David came over to me and squeezed my hand.

"Who wants a drink?" Justin called from the bar in the family room. We went to join Justin, my heels clicking over the new mosaic tile Suzanne had put in the entryway.

"I'll have a vodka martini since you're pouring," David said. He sat down on one of the barstools.

"And you, Robin?" Justin asked, "There's a nice Chardonnay back here."

"That sounds great."

"Let's have drinks in here," Justin said. "Alaina will be tempted enough for the wine at dinner. We don't have to tease her too much."

"I can't believe you have another one on the way already." David said.

"We've been busy," Justin replied, smiling.

"Seriously, Justin, when do you have anytime for yourself? And how the hell do you keep the kids from ruining all your things?"

"David!" I said aghast.

"What?" David said, looking at me.

"Don't worry, Robin," Justin laughed in his easygoing way. "Listen, David, kids are messy, whiny, and they do get into everything. They're also full of fun and love. I look forward all day to coming home to be with them. They smile, and hug me, and yell "Daddy" when I walk in the door. They run to me with happiness bursting from within them, just because I'm me. Damn! They make me feel like the most important man on earth. And you know what?" Justin said, looking into David's eyes, "I can always move my stuff."

"Has the meeting been called to order?" Alaina said as she walked in.

"I'll order you a Perrier with a splash of grapefruit juice," Justin replied, winking at Alaina.

"Gee thanks," Alaina said ruefully, "I'll just pretend it's some exotic island drink."

"That's my girl." Justin handed Alaina the drink. He had topped it with a little umbrella sticking out and a maraschino cherry floating on top.

"Hey, I'll have one of those," Miles said, as he pointed to Alaina's drink. "Throw some vodka in mine though." We all laughed.

"Where are mom and the twins?" Justin asked his dad, as he handed him his drink."

"She took them upstairs to the den where she had some toys put away for them.

"More stuff?" Alaina groaned.

"Let her have her fun. Wait to you see the clothes she bought them." Alaina groaned again, and Justin laughed. I watched David. His eyes had a faraway look to them.

How odd, I thought, they never looked that reflective before.

"Dinner is served," Marie announced. David came over, and squeezed my shoulders in a one-arm hug.

As we drove toward my parents' home, I thought about the cute picture David made with Kenneth and Kayla both on his lap, listening to a story. Kenneth, bored with the book, suddenly pushed David over and started climbing on his back. Kayla laughed and joined in until they were a tangle of arms and legs. David laughed and yelled to Justin and me for help. I came over and David pulled me into the melee. I yelped and he yelled, "Pile on Aunt Robin!" Justin came to my rescue.

I had never seen David so relaxed looking. His hair was all mussed as he laughed, and held Kayla high up in the air and listened to her screech "Make me fly, Uncle David."

"So was that two pieces of pie I saw you eat, or three?" David said, interrupting my thoughts and poking me in the stomach.

"Look who's talking ? Wasn't it you taking a third helping of stuffing?" I said, as I poked him back.

"Hey, careful," David said laughing and grabbed for my hand. "No defense, Robin, Marie sure makes incredible stuffing."

"I'll pass along the compliment next time I speak to your mom," I replied. "Justin and Alaina seem very happy," I said nonchalantly.

"Yes they do," David replied just as vague, but then he continued,

"Still, I don't know how Justin can relax at home with all that craziness."

"It's not craziness, David. It's called having a family. You make it sound like he's running a children's home."

"I'm sure it feels like it," David replied laughing.

"You did hear what Justin said?" I asked softly.

"Yes, I did." David sounded as if he still couldn't believe Justin felt that way. It sounded incredible to him. "Still," he added, "Maybe there is some truth to what Justin says." We drove the rest of the way deep in our own thoughts.

# Chapter 11

As Jill and I walked down Fifth Avenue, we talked Christmas. We had lunch at a restaurant above Rockefeller Center, and watched the skaters below. It was forty degrees and I watched as the skaters blew out cold air. It felt good to be warm. Jill and I sat by the window drinking our hot chocolate.

"What did you get David for Christmas?" Jill asked.

"I had that picture Douglas took of us at Stuart's and Celia's anniversary party blown up, and framed for his desk at work.

"That was a great picture of you two."

"Thanks, I want to get David some cufflinks as well. What did you get Tyler?"

"The usual gift certificate to that plant store he loves. Cufflinks sound like a good idea. Tyler really needs some. Do you know what David bought you for Christmas yet?" Jill asked.

"No. He's been walking around like the cat that swallowed the canary, lately. I know he's got something planned that he thinks is pretty special. I've been practicing my 'How did you know I've always wanted this' expressions." Jill laughed.

"If I know David, it's probably something he wants rather than you, so it's a good idea to practice."

"Jill!" I kicked her under the table.

"Ow! Well, Tyler's not any better. Remember what he got me last year?"

"I remember. The leaf print jacket, I thought it was kind of pretty."

"You would. Well, this year I didn't take any chances. I saw a beautiful pair of diamond earrings with a bracelet to match in my favorite jewelry store catalog. I tore the page out and put it in his briefcase. If he doesn't get that hint , I give up. I'll be buying myself presents for Christmas from now on." I laughed.

"Whatever David gets me I'll love."

"Only if it has four feet and a tail. You know all you want is a puppy, ever since you've seen Joanne's."

"That is one thing I won't get." I sighed as I remembered David's reaction to Joanne's puppy.

"You wouldn't want to put it in a kennel when we go on the cruise, anyway." Jill squeezed my hand. "Come, if we're going to get any Christmas shopping done today, we'd better go"

"Agreed," I said, as we left for the shops.

I had just told Jill about the lovely lamp I'd found for my parents when my eye caught sight of a breath-taking velvet gown. It was long and had a darling jacket.

"Try it on, Robin," Jill urged. "It will be beautiful for New Year's Eve." Our husbands were taking us for dinner and dancing.

"Okay." I modeled it for Jill, and we both pronounced it perfect both for New Year's Eve and the formal dinner on the cruise. I bought it, and told the sales lady to have it delivered. We next searched for gifts for the guys. I found the perfect set of cufflinks for David. Jill bought some for Tyler.

"Tyler will look stylish on this cruise if it kills me," Jill said. I laughed, Tyler was so easygoing that he wore whatever Jill bought him. David was harder to shop for, but I thought he would like the cufflinks, and he needed a new pair.

Jill dragged me to one of her favorite shops. I looked at sweaters. She found a lovely crème-colored gown for New Year's Eve that fit her beautifully.

As we walked down the street, I spotted a toy store. It was my turn to drag Jill inside. I found an adorable doll for Kayla and a truck set for Kenneth. The set was cute. It had a dump truck and a bulldozer. I picked up a second one just as Jill came over, arms loaded with toys for her nephews.

"Who's the other one for?" Jill asked knowingly.

"It's for Max," I said. I tried to sound like it was no big deal. Jill looked at me, not fooled for a moment.

"Robin!" she began, but I interrupted.

"Jill, it's nothing. I just want to make sure he has at least one present. What if Christmas is like Halloween, and Max doesn't even know it's a holiday?" Jill looked at me, not sure what to say.

"You said he had Thanksgiving at the Johnsons' daughter's house. I'm sure the Johnsons celebrate Christmas if they celebrate Thanksgiving." I had seen Max a few times since Halloween and had spoken with Mrs. Johnson. She told me all about her daughter, Mildred, and how she made such wonderful Holiday meals.

"That's true. He may have a nice Christmas dinner, but that doesn't mean he'll get any presents."

Jill continued to look at me strangely.

"Does David know how close you're getting to this boy?" I was surprised by such a direct question.

"What do you mean? He's just a boy I see at the park. Don't make too much out of this, Jill."

She paused before answering softly. "I won't if you won't"

Jill went home after the toy store. I was tired but happy, I had gotten all my Christmas shopping done. I began to wrap the presents I had bought. When I got to Max's present, I stopped and looked at it for a moment. Maybe Jill was right. Maybe I should tell David more about Max. However, he doesn't want to hear about him, I reminded myself and what would I say. I mean, he was just a little boy I saw at the park. I was getting lost in my own mind conversations when the phone rang. I jumped. I answered it in a hoarse voice.

"Hello?"

"Hi dear, you sound strange. Please don't tell me you're getting sick." My mother's voice was filled with a mixture of concern and exasperation.

"Oh, no, Mom. I was just lost in thought. How are you?"

"Fine, dear, I just wanted to know at what time you'll be coming on Christmas Day, so I can plan dinner accordingly."

"Oh. We'll probably be leaving here around eleven, so I guess twelve-thirty-ish?"

"That's fine. I'll plan dinner for around three-o'clock." She paused for a moment. "Are you sure everything's alright, Robin? Is David okay?"

"We're fine, Mom, really. It's just, well, have I ever mentioned a boy I've met in the park?"

"A what? A boy? What kind of boy? Robin, you're not thinking of disgracing this family by having an affair. David is so wonderful. He treats you like gold. How could you be thinking ...."

"Mom, it's a little boy I'm talking about. A four-year-old boy named Max."

"Robin, I'm not following this at all. Why in the world are you befriending a little boy? Is he the child of a friend of yours?"

"No." *How in the world do I explain this?* I thought. "I met Max when I was feeding the birds in the park."

"You spend too much time at that park! You should be taking care of your home."

"Mom, please listen, this is important to me." I didn't know why it was important for my mother to understand this, but I felt I needed to try, and convey my feelings to someone.

"I'm listening."

"Max is a sweet little boy. An elderly couple takes care of him. I really don't know much about him. He likes to help me feed the birds, and he's a monkey when it comes to climbing." I tried to sound casual and light but my mother wasn't buying it.

"Does David know about this boy?"

"Yes, David knows about Max. I mean, he knows that I have seen him in the park."

"Good! That's all he should know. There's nothing else to know. You listen to me, Robin. If it makes you happy to see this boy at the park, fine: talk to him there. If this couple who cares for him doesn't mind. I know you, Robin, better than you know yourself. You've always been this 'save the world' child. Well, this will no longer work anymore. You have a husband who works hard to give you a beautiful home, and he doesn't need to hear about your crazy ideas when he gets home. You leave this

Max at the park and don't get anymore emotionally involved than you already are. If you need a cause, why don't you get more involved in your women's league? They do charitable work that should be perfect for you."

"Yes, fine, that's a good idea," I answered. I knew I would hear more arguments if I didn't agree. "Mom, I need to go, David should be home any minute."

"I'll see you on Christmas day, Robin, and remember what I said."

I wrapped Max's present and then finished the others. I went out to the greenhouse. I needed to relax. My plants understood me better than anyone else. An hour later, I felt better. David came in just as I closed the French door. I went over and gave him a big hello kiss. He smiled and went to hug me then stopped, grimacing at seeing how dirty I was. I laughed and went to wash up.

"How was work?" I asked as David sat down for dinner. I had already put the leftover chicken and rice on the table. I passed David the salad I had just made, and sat down too,

"Quiet, no one's in a business mood with Christmas so near." He sounded annoyed. To David, banking was his hobby as well as his work. He couldn't understand when his colleagues didn't show the same enthusiasm as he did.

"Well, everyone's ready for a little break," I said soothingly. "Is Stuart taking everyone to lunch on Friday?" Stuart usually had a big Christmas party for the senior staff, but Celia had flown to Paris the week before for the Holidays. Stuart was joining her the coming weekend in Paris. He had decided to take only the senior staff to lunch, this year.

"He'll probably give us our bonus then. You know Stuart, he likes to make a big show out of it. The old ham," David said affectionately. I smiled. David was lucky to have a boss he was so fond of.

"So did you go shopping with Jill?" David asked, changing the subject.

"Yes, I wrapped everything and put it in the closet."

"I saw the toy store bag. We'll have to hold on to the twins' gifts for a while. They won't be back until after New Year's. I guess we'll see them before we leave for the Caribbean."

Justin and Alaina were in Seattle staying with Alaina's parents for the holidays. David's parents were in Spain for the holidays, staying with an old friend of David's father. I hesitated wondering if I should mention Max's gift. My mother might say something to David and that would be a mess. I moved slowly, feeling David out.

"I bought Max a little something for Christmas," I said in a casual way.

David paused for a moment.

"Who's Max? Oh, yes, that kid from the park, right?" He continued to eat and didn't say anything. I looked at him astounded. Well, I thought to myself, talk about making a mountain out of a molehill. I totally relaxed. What were Jill and my mother worrying about? David couldn't care less. He was right, Max was just a little kid I happened to know. Big deal, a Christmas present. It was no different than the gift I gave Bill, the doorman.

I cleared the dishes as David went into the living room to read the paper. I put the dishes in the sink, and then I stopped. That was exactly what David thought, that Max meant nothing more to me than just any other kid in the park. David thought Max was just like the birds I fed at the park. I gave them bread and they were happy, and I was happy to have helped take care of them. Is that how I felt about Max? I bring him a present and he's happy and I feel good that I made his day a little brighter? Yes! I told myself.

I loaded the dishwasher and pushed any other stray feelings away. There was nothing to think about. My mother made it sound as if it were David or Max. Jill said the same, but it wasn't that at all. All that drama. David was right, this was nothing, nothing!

I retold myself this over and over as I listened to the whirl of the dishwasher. Each cycle of its wash and rinse convincing me it was true.

# Chapter 12

I awoke to the delicious feeling of kisses showered all over my face. I opened my eyes and stared into David's shining hazel eyes. He was beaming as if he had single-handedly accomplished some monumental event.

"Merry Christmas, sleepy head!" he said, as he lay down beside me. He was holding a little black remote control of some sort. David stared at me, smiling. The look said, 'hurry up and ask me what I'm holding. He was so excited. I loved it when David was in these playful moods, so I obliged him.

"What's that? Is it for me?" I exclaimed, sounding overly joyous. He laughed, happy with my enthusiasm.

"Not so fast, greedy one, maybe it is and maybe it isn't." I pouted appropriately. David laughed again.

"You'll have to do better than that, my love." He kissed my neck, and held the remote out of reach.

"Have you been a good girl all year? You know Santa sees you when you're naughty and nice." I tried to grab the remote and he pulled it back. He bit my ear, as he whispered, "Of course, a little naughty is nice."

I pushed him back on the bed as he laughed and continued to keep the remote out of reach. I sat on his chest with my arms folded, "David," I said in my most mock stern voice.

"Alright, alright." He grinned. "What did you want most this year?" I must have looked puzzled because he continued, "I think it's the only thing Joanne has that you want." My face turned from puzzled to shock. He couldn't mean a puppy! I couldn't believe David would get me a puppy. I didn't hear any barking. And why was he holding a remote? David smiled at me, looking very pleased with himself. I didn't want to guess, and then be wrong.

"It's not. Is it a puppy?"

"Yep," he said.

"Oh, David!" I screamed, "Where is it? I don't hear any barking. Is it on the patio? Let me see it." I made to climb off him but he held my arm.

"Hold on, the puppy will come to us." Now I was confused. David pressed something on the remote, and I heard yapping. Into the room came this small mechanical puppy. It looked amazingly real. I felt my heart sink, but I tried to smile.

David, caught up in his surprise, didn't notice my disappointment.

"Look Robbie," he said, as he moved some of the controls. "See, this makes him walk and this one makes him bark. And watch this." David pressed another button and the puppy spun. I sank onto the bed as David got up and picked up the puppy. He put it in my arms. The fur was soft to the touch. Where there should have been skin and bones, I felt the metal and springs. The puppy tried to lick my face as David moved the remote.

"Can you believe it, Robbie? He's actually licking your face, your face is wet! Isn't that unbelievable? I saw it in a Japanese catalog and knew it would be perfect for you." David pressed another button and the dog turned off. "The perfect dog. Here to play with you, and then you can turn it off when you've had enough. Don't have to feed it, or walk it, or worry about it when we go on trips, it's the perfect pet." David was happy. What could I say? I thanked him then I saw a black box on the floor. David followed my glance and saw the box too. He grinned.

"See, even drops things like a real dog." David picked up the box and brought it to me. I opened the box and gasped. Inside the box was the most exquisite strand of pearls I have ever seen. I lifted the pearls up to see them shimmer in the light.

"Just a little something to go with the dog." He smiled at me, full of hope that he had pleased me. I put the dog and pearls down and jumped into his arms kissing him deeply and thanking him the way he liked best.

After some added time in bed, I went to make coffee as David showered. I put the puppy on the counter. I pressed the remote and he yapped and licked me. I patted him, sighed, and scratched his ear, as I said, "I guess you wouldn't want to spend a week in a kennel when we left on our cruise. Not to mention the trip to Greece that we have planned for the summer." I created a mental imagine of placing a dog in the kennel, realized it would probably ruin the trip for me, and David would be angry. "Yes," I thought, and patted the mechanical dog again. "Ours is definitely not the lifestyle for a real dog." I looked at the pearls sitting next to the dog and I squelched any rebellious thoughts, remembering to be thankful for what I had. Feeling happier, I got out the special muffins and croissants I had bought yesterday at the bakery. I also placed my present for David on his plate.

David came in dressed casually in Dockers and a sweater. He patted the dog and sat down eyeing the gift.

"A present for me? You shouldn't have," he said smugly. I playfully pulled his hair as he opened it. He looked at the photo of us and smiled.

"Beautiful, It will look great on my desk." He stared at it a minute longer "You did look special that night. I was the envy of all men." It was supposed to be a compliment to me, but in the way it was said, I knew David was congratulating himself. It made me feel a little like Eliza Doolittle from *My Fair Lady*, but I kissed and thanked him anyway. He then opened the cufflinks Jill had helped me pick out.
"Very nice choice, Robbie, and I could use a new pair for the cruise." He kissed me as I poured him some coffee.

After we ate, I went and took a shower and finished packing. We were staying at my parents overnight. It took a few minutes to throw in some clothes and their gifts.

We left for Connecticut a little after eleven. There wasn't too much traffic, everyone was either at home or in church. David and I were both brought up Lutheran, but neither of our families were religious. We were at my parents' home by twelve-thirty.

"I can't believe Dad hung the Christmas lights up this year, since none of the kids will be here," I said. My brothers were both spending Christmas with their spouses' families since they were here last Christmas.

"Maybe your Dad was in a festive mood." We parked on the driveway and I opened the door with my key.

"There's my little girl," Dad said, as he got up from his lounge chair and hugged me and shook hands with David.

"Corrine, the kids are here!" Dad shouted to the kitchen.

"Yes, dear, I'm coming." Mom wiped her hands on her apron when she came into the hallway. She looked lovely in her red dress with her hair bobbed softly around her face. Her hair, with a little help from her salon, was still blond, like mine. She is in wonderful shape, and I as looked at her, it was impossible to believe she was in her late sixties. I gave her a warm hug and kiss. She hugged me and then, David.

"Merry Christmas, darlings. David, come give me your jacket. Can I get you a drink? Sit down." David let my mom lead him away and I slipped my arm through my dad's as we walked into the living room. My mom had David seated and was getting him a gin and tonic.

"Make me one too, dear," Dad said as he sat back in his chair. I sat next to David on the sofa. Mom brought the guys their drinks.

"Look what David gave me for Christmas, Mom." I lifted the pearls around my neck. My mother came over for a closer look.

"Exquisite! David, you have such impeccable taste." David beamed. Mom smiled at him. "Now you just relax while we girls get some snacks for you two. Robin, help me in the kitchen." I sighed and got up again. David laughed and slapped my bottom as I moved around him. David thought it was hilarious how my mother caters to the males in my family. I'm sure David still had hope that more of her trait would rub off on me.

I followed Mom into the kitchen as Dad asked David about his stocks.

"Dear, why don't you get the caviar out of the fridge? Here are some toast points I just made." I placed the caviar and toast on a silver tray. Mom tasted the soup. She covered it and turned the burner to warm.

"Where's Maria?" I asked. "Did you give her the day off?' Maria was my mother's housekeeper.

"Why of course, do you think I'd make her work on Christmas? You know Spanish people like to spend Christmas in church. Maria helped me cook yesterday. When she finished cleaning, I let her leave for mass." I winced when my mother made the Spanish people and church comment. I hated how she grouped people by race or nationality. Still, I didn't say anything. We had had the discussion before and it had always gone nowhere.

I walked into the living room with the caviar and set it down on the coffee table. David and Dad were still discussing stocks. Dad was telling David about a new investment, and how well it was paying off. He teased David that this tip was part of his Christmas gift to us.

"Speaking of gifts, did Robin mention our new addition to the family?" My mother walked in with a tray of imported cheeses just as David said this. She stopped and almost dropped the tray. Dad thankfully saved it and put it down next to the caviar.

"Robin! Oh darling! I'm going to be a grandma again. When are you due?" David looked at her as if she had lost her mind.
"Oh, God, no, Corrine." David sounded horrified. I glared at him and he came over and quickly hugged me. "Sorry, Robin, that didn't come out right. Your mom just shocked me. We're both not ready for that, right, sweetheart?" I didn't get a chance to answer.

"There you go, Corrine, always jumping to conclusions, let the man finish his sentence. Now, what addition David?" Dad said.

"I'm sorry, David, you just caught me by surprise, please finish, dear."

"Robin's wanted a dog." This time, my dad interrupted.

"What do you want a dog for, Robin? They are such a nuisance, barking and chewing things."

"Yes, really, Robin," my mother chimed in. "How is David going to be able to relax when he gets home with a dog jumping around. I hope you didn't give in to this fool notion of Robin's, David. You shouldn't let her take advantage of your kind nature." I was now biting my lip to stop myself from screaming.

"No, no Corrine." I could tell David was enjoying this immensely. "What I bought her was an electronic dog. It works by remote and it feels like a real dog! It also walks, barks, and licks like a real dog." My dad was amazed.

"By George! Where did you find that contraption?"

"I ordered it from Japan" David said smugly. He was extremely pleased by my parents' reaction."

"David, you are so clever," my mom gushed. "Robin, I hope you know how lucky you are. To go to all that trouble to get you a dog and one you don't even have to take care of."

My mom made this sound like such a good thing. I wanted to scream, "The reason you get a dog is to take care of it!" Instead, I looked at David. "It was a very sweet gift and David's right, it is quite amazing," I said.

"And when you go on your cruise, you can just turn him off. That's what I call a great dog," My dad added.

This reminded my mother of the cruise. "Have you started shopping for clothes yet, Robin? You should go to some of the shops here. They have some of the most darling outfits." Mom and I went back to the kitchen while David told Dad about this company he ordered the dog from.

We finished putting dinner on the table and called in the men. My dad brought in a bottle of wine he had just brought up from the wine cellar. Dad poured the wine as David sat down where my mother told him to.

"Now you men relax as Robin and I serve the soup." I thought, ruefully, that David and Dad had done nothing but relax for the last two hours, but there was no gain in saying that to my mother. My grandmother was the same way, and I suppose so was my great grandmother. We were here to serve our men. Men worked hard to make a living and deserved to do nothing when at home. I'd like to think I had risen above this catering to men attitude, but, in truth, was I really so different? Granted, David didn't expect me to have a home cooked meal every night, or for me to meet him at the door with a drink in hand, but there were other things. Even with the freedoms I had acquired over my female ancestors, there were still too many constraints.

I looked at David happily eating his soup, my mother hanging on his every word until my father said something, and then her attention would totally focus on him. I sat down with my own soup, silenced by my conflicting thoughts.

After the delicious dinner, David and my father went to my father's study for an after-dinner cigar. My mother filled me in on all the happenings with our relatives. She said she and my Aunt Margaret (my mother's sister) were trying to get my dad and Uncle Hubert to agree on a trip to Australia. That is one of the few places my parents had not been yet. I was surprised that my father didn't want to go. He normally loved to travel.

"We are getting older, Robin. Australia is a big trip." I smiled and remembered that my father had said the same thing when they went to China three years ago. They had a marvelous time. I reminded my mother of this.

"Oh, yes, that's right. I had forgotten that your father was leery of that trip too. Well, I will remind him, and maybe he'll agree to Australia." My mother continued to load the dishwasher as I put food away.

"Speaking of getting older," my mother began. I tensed, knowing what was coming next.

"Were we speaking of getting older? I don't remember. They say that the memory is the first to go," I quipped, buying time.

"Now, Robin, don't get saucy. As I was saying, I almost had hoped when David spoke of a Christmas surprise. Especially, after that strange conversation we had about that boy in the park. I think maybe that's your whole problem in a nutshell. I meant it when I said I wanted to be a grandmother again." That was so like mom to think she can wrap all my feelings and thoughts together, and then tell me what to do to with them.

"Mom, you know we're not ready yet."

"Who's not ready yet?" My mother's look said she knew where the delay was coming from. "Robin, you know I would never say anything against David. And, I've always believed that you should abide by your husband's feelings. You should never push a man to do something he's not ready for. Still, in this case, time is an issue, Robin."

"Yes, Mother, I know all this." I interrupted, my tone had an edge. Thankfully, Mom decided to let it drop, but with one last comment.

"Fine, fine." My mother threw up her hands before drying them on the dish towel. "You know, dear, there are ways to get a man to do something without a confrontation. That's how I managed your father all these years. Let the man know he's king of the castle, and he'll be happy. Once he's happy, it's easy to slip in a few things you want done." Here, she stopped and paused. I could see her trying to find the words.

*Don't say it,* I begged silently. *Don't say it.*

"Darling," she said, grasping my arm. "You are pleasing him in bed, aren't you?"

I stared at her just a moment. I knew not to answer would lead to more incriminations later.

"Yes, Mother."

"That's how a smart woman gets what she needs, dear." She smiled, as if she has solved all my problems. I turned and left trying to swallow the last part of my dinner, which was now threatening to come back up.

Thankfully, that discussion was left in the kitchen as we rejoined the men in the living room. My dad was lighting a fire, and David was assisting. I took this opportunity to quietly slip upstairs and retrieve the gifts I had brought my parents.

"Robin dear, this is lovely!" My mother exclaimed as she opened the antique lamp I had bought her.

"It was originally Thomas Jefferson's. I found it at this exclusive antique store in The Village."

"It will look perfect in your father's study . Don't you think so, darling?" My father was examining the Rolex I had picked out for him.

"Beautiful watch, Robbie, I could use a new one, too." I beamed happily, with this one small success.

"Robin, this is for both of you." I opened the envelope my mother handed me and saw a card for an all-inclusive weekend in the mountains.

"Thank you. That's a wonderful present!"

My mother smiled.

"I know how busy David is, it's nice to have a weekend getaway. They have wonderful tennis there. You two can book the weekend any time."

"Thank you, Corrine, that was very thoughtful of you both." My mother beamed at David's praise for her gift.

We sat around the fire reminiscing about Christmas past. Mom and I made hot toddies and popcorn and we watched *"It's A Wonderful Life,"* one of my dad's favorite movies. Soon after the movie was over, David and I went up to bed.

David and I cuddled in the guest room as the winter winds blew outside. It was a lovely Christmas. The conversation in the kitchen had already faded. It made me curious about myself, though. I never really thought about being manipulative in the bedroom. I reminded myself that David and I were open enough to discuss things that were important to us. I mean, if there was really something I wanted, I was sure David would agree. Then I thought about the chickadee and the mechanical dog. I winced and tried not to think anymore.

We left my parents after morning brunch. My mother kissed me, and said, "Remember dear, you are the key to family harmony." I smiled tightly and I hugged her goodbye.

A week before our cruise, I decided to go to the park. It was a cool sixty degrees and I had the feeling Max might be there. I wanted to know how his Christmas went.

It was such a lovely day, I walked the ten short blocks. Max was on the playground. He wore a worn light blue windbreaker. It was the same jacket I saw him in when I gave him his Christmas present weeks ago. I thought it strange then that he didn't have on a heavier coat. The thought that he didn't have a heavier coat made my stomach tighten. *He's wearing that jacket because it's warm today,* I reasoned. I was only wearing a heavy sweater.

"Hi Max," I called. He jumped off his swing and ran to me.

"Robin!" he answered excitedly. I bent down and gave him a hug. Mrs. Johnson was sitting alone on the bench.

"Hi, Mrs. Johnson, where's Mr. Johnson today?"

"Hello, Miss Robin." She insisted on calling me this, even though I told her "Robin" was fine.

"He's feeling poorly today. I brought Max out here so he could rest. Beautiful day, ain't it?"

"Yes, it is, did you have a nice Christmas?"

"Yes, real nice, my daughter Mildred cooked a wonderful dinner, right Max?"

"Yeah," Max answered, without enthusiasm.

"See my new ball, Robin? Look! It bounces up high." Max picked up the ball and showed me how high it bounced. Mrs. Johnson smiled at him.

"That's great, Max. Do you want to play catch?"

"Sure." We played catch. Later, I pushed him on the swings while Mrs. Johnson dozed on the bench.

"Did you have fun at Mildred's, Max?" I asked.

"I guess," he said, then hesitated. "I don't think Mildred likes me much."

"Why do you say that, Max?"

"She gives me mean looks."

"Does she hurt you, Max?" I asked tentatively.

"No, she just looks mean. She cooks good though." I breathed a sigh of relief. I guess the looks couldn't be any worse than Mr. Johnson yelling at him all the time.

"I don't think she means anything by those looks, Max, don't let them bother you," I tried to reassure him.

"I guess," he said. "Want to play in the sand with my trucks?" His face was all smiles again. I saw the two trucks I had given him for Christmas sitting by the bench. I was glad Mrs. Johnson thought to bring them to the park.

"Sure," I said. We played in the sand while I tried to explain to Max that I was going on a cruise. He asked me a lot of questions. He seemed sad that I was leaving. I promised to bring him back a present, which made him happy.

I left Max after Mrs. Johnson had awakened. I felt good, happy that Max had had a nice Christmas. I felt better about the Johnsons, too. I went home ready to leave on my trip with a light heart.

# Chapter 13

As I listened to the coffee grinder, my thoughts were already traveling on the cruise ship. David slept soundly. Our flight to Florida was not until one o'clock. I looked at the clock. It was only eight-thirty. I squelched my excitement, and planned what I would wear on the plane.

Jill and I had bought out the stores the week before. We had a wonderful time at *Saks* buying the latest in cruising attire. I even chanced to pick up some things for David, which to my amazement, he liked.

I looked out the window and watched the wind. I shivered. It was as if I was stood outside. I placed my long suede jacket and matching gloves ready at the door. In spite of my decision not to , I thought about Max in his worn, thin windbreaker, and then forced myself to stop. I went into the bedroom to take a bath. David was sitting up in bed, smiling.

"My first day of vacation, Robbie, come here and let's get it off to a fabulous beginning." I laughed.

"I was just going to take a bath, want to join me?'

"You join me first."

I made to crawl over him, but he grabbed me and pulled me down onto his chest. He put his hands deep into my hair and pulled me to his lips.

"MMM, now that's a great way to get my morning coffee. I need to start getting you up before me more often."

"Really. And how do you propose to do that?"

"I think I know a few spots that are sure to wake you." He then proceeded to show me those spots as if I didn't know where they were. I began to pant. Sensations of pleasure erupted throughout my body.

"Don't stop," I gasped. "Then again," David laughed, "this method of getting coffee may be a lot more strenuous than just making it." I threw a pillow at him and told him to finish what he started.

After a nice long soak in the Jacuzzi, I made some breakfast for both us. David leisurely drank coffee and read the paper. I, instead, ran around trying to remember all the last minute things I needed. David, of course, was packed, his suitcases next to the front door.

We left at eleven o'clock. Bill hailed a taxi for us. David didn't want to leave his Lexus at the airport for a week. We arrived at the airport with time to spare. I saw Jill as she ran toward me, arms opened wide. We hugged in excitement. To onlookers, it probably looked as if we hadn't seen each other in years not just two days ago.

Our flight arrived on time. Jill and I occupied ourselves on the flight looking at Jill's book about the Western Caribbean. The men lounged in their seats as the stewardess brought snacks and drinks.

"First class is the only way to go," David said, as he sipped his martini. I smiled. I was glad he was relaxing. David could be a bear on airplanes, especially if the flight was delayed. My stomach contracted just thinking of the time when we flew to Switzerland. There was a three-hour delay. I think David yelled at every person in charge for the entire three hours.

The plane landed in sunny Florida. I took a deep breath of warm air, glad I wore a short-sleeved blouse under the suede jacket that was now draped over my arm. The cruise ship had a limo van waiting for passengers. The porter brought our bags over and placed them carefully in the trunk. I gave David my look that said, "Give him a nice tip" David grumbled and handed him a twenty. The porter beamed at us and walked away.

We soon arrived at the ship. I smiled when I saw it. It was beautiful. It was a new ship, second voyage out. We smiled for the entrance photo, even though David hates to take those photos. We walked past the calypso band and into the lounge, where drinks and caviar were being served. There was a lunch buffet with an ice sculpture of a blue whale. The water blowing from his blowhole was suspended into magical ice crystals. I was too excited to eat. David gave me a look, so I took a little fruit. We all toasted from the bottle of champagne David ordered, clinking our glasses together.

After we unpacked, we all met in a different lounge and discussed the activity schedule over drinks. I should say Jill and I discussed it. Tyler and David were talking about the casino and planning, "Where to invest." This reminded Tyler of a stock he had just bought. It was rumored the stock would grow by leaps and bounds. That was all David needed to hear. He left us to call his broker, before the ship sailed. Jill and I smiled at each other knowingly. The stock market was usually the only gambling both our husbands were interested in.

"Wow, Robin, look at all the treatments offered at the spa and salon. We must have a mud wrap. I heard salt scrubs leave your skin glowing." I made a face at Jill and she hurriedly turned the page. "Take a mud wrap with me and I'll do the aroma therapy with you, deal?"
"Deal," I said. We laughed. We talked. Interspersed with laughter, we talked. Waiters carried trays of canapés and refilled our wine glasses. The guys suggested a stroll on deck. I grabbed a shrimp as we left the lounge deck.

We went out onto the deck. The sea breezes hit us with gusto and I sighed, delighted. David put his arm around my shoulder and pulled me in for a spontaneous kiss. I grinned up at him. He rarely showed affection around other people. Tyler, who was much more open, held Jill in a long embrace. David saw this too. *Good,* I thought. *Maybe they'll have a positive influence on my sometimes stoic husband.*

It only took a day and a half to reach the Bahamas; the first stop through the Caribbean. We took advantage of the many activities the ship had to offer. Sometimes, we paired off in couples, other times it was just girls and boys. At night, we all met for dinner, dancing, and sometimes the evening show, if the guys could sit through it without groaning.

In the morning, we docked in the Bahamas. We made our way leisurely down to the island. We had been warned about the many Bahamians that we would encounter as soon as we walked down the gangway, and they were there. David had also given me his own personal warning that he didn't want to see me buying all their crap, as he so elegantly put it.

I braced myself as we walked down the gangway. It is always a shock, the sight of all the children, begging us to buy their trinkets. I thought of Max, and almost lost my resolve. However, I reminded myself, that I was determined this would be a good trip, no fights between David and myself.

Tyler, who was more like me, bought some beaded necklaces, ignoring the look Jill gave him. David didn't even seem to see the people. He talked to me about doing some jet skiing.

Then almost as if I conjured him up after thinking of Max, I saw a little Bahamian boy. He was holding tight to the skirt of a girl, who looked to be his ten-year-old sister or cousin. The little boy had some kind of burn mark that covered half his forearm. He looked at me with forlorn eyes as his sister or cousin tried to sell me beaded bracelets. I stood transfixed.

David realized that I wasn't holding his hand anymore, and turned to find me. He scowled when he saw me. Then he looked down at the children, as if he just realized there were people selling things. He saw the boy. The boy smiled at David and showed gapped teeth. I thought David would grab my arm in a second and propel me forward, but he didn't, he just stood for a moment staring at the boy. He seemed almost in a trance until he heard Tyler call his name. He grabbed ten dollars from his billfold and gave it to the little boy. The sister quickly put it away.

I turned astonished eyes at David.

"Don't say anything," he grunted. He grabbed my hand and pulled me through the crowd.

We had a wonderful day in the Bahamas. We rented jet skis and skied our way around the shore. I was on with David, and Jill was with Tyler. Tyler, the outdoorsman of the group, had been on skis a few times before and was zipping around with ease. David, who can learn anything quickly when he wants too, soon followed close behind.

After a couple of hours with beach breaks, we were more than ready to turn in our jet skis for some piña coladas at the outside cafes. We all tried the jerk chicken with rice and chutney, and leisurely ate while watching the sun worshippers on the beach. Some people with more energy to expend were playing volleyball and Frisbee.

The afternoon was spent at the outdoor marketplace that seemed to go on forever. The guys really did think it went on forever, they left us to go into a Tavern. But not before leaving us with strict warnings. "Don't leave the marketplace! We will meet you in one hour in front of this tavern, don't be late!" David talked to me as if I had just seen a city for the first time. I knew he was afraid I would innocently wander into some lurid place that quickly disposed of tourists. I smiled reassuringly at him.

"I'll take care of her, David," Jill said. We walked away as Jill muttered, "Honestly, you'd think he never lets you out of the bedroom." I playfully hit her with my newly purchased handbag.

I picked up trinkets here and there, including an adorable doll for Kayla. Now I just needed something cute for Kenneth. I spotted a toy wooden boat two tables over and quickly bought it. I didn't like the look the lady I bought it from gave me. She had a smirk on her round face that told me I should have haggled better. I was actually surprised I could do it at all. The only thing that helped me was that I knew the Bahamians were insulted if I didn't at least try.

We picked up the guys. They were in the middle of a heavy game of darts.

"Oh, Robin! I knew we shouldn't have left them," Jill said in her best down-trodden voice. "Look what all the gambling and cavorting have lowered them to, darts in a tavern! Why, next they'll be searching for a billiard room." I giggled.

"Ha, ha. We'll see who has the last laugh tonight, wench, when I've got you where I want you," Tyler said, and pulled Jill down on his lap and held her tight.

"Oh, you brute," Jill exclaimed playfully as she pummeled him with her fist. David watched smiling tightly. I could tell that all this public display of affection made him uncomfortable. He was trying hard to seem nonchalant about it for Jill and Tyler's sake. I squeezed his shoulder to acknowledge I knew his feelings. He smiled up at me for real.

That night, we set off for Jamaica. I sat at the table on our balcony as David checked his e-mail on his laptop. The maid had just delivered my dress for the evening. I had had it repressed, it wrinkled on the trip over. David had also sent his tux to be pressed and his shoes polished.

We sat watching the water as it streamed by. David sipped his wine and then pointed out a school of dolphins off to the right. They were tricky to see in the moonlight. I laughed and clapped my hands when one jumped higher than the others.

David squeezed my hand and gave me that look I knew so well.

I glanced at my watch, plenty of time before our late dinner. David held me close as we walked to the king-sized bed. He pushed me slowly back. He always has total control when he drinks, but now he had a hazy look in his eyes, a combination of the day in the sun and numerous drinks throughout the day. He grinned at me saucily. I grinned back and thought we would  probably order room service tonight.


"We missed you two at dinner last night" Jill said, as she winked at David. David turned red, and I gave Jill a "not funny" look. Jill laughed. Tyler and Jill were so relaxed and easy-going that we didn't need to keep tabs on each other all the time. That was why we enjoyed vacationing with them. David varied between needing to be in constant control, knowing what was going on at all times, and then changing the plan at the last second. The rest of us really needed to be laid-back.

Jill and I thought we should watch the class on culinary demonstrations. The guys thought they would enter the golf putting contests. David is a wonderful golfer. He forgot all about Jill's teasing as he relished the chance to show off his skill.

As we walked toward the culinary class, we passed the children's camp. I peeked in through the window. The kids seemed to be having fun. I almost wished I could join them. I watched a few eight and nine-year-old girls make sun catchers with a counselor. A group of boys were building boats and birdhouses. I was happy to see that when a couple of the girls were finished with their sun catchers, they went to the boys table and started banging away at the boats as well.

Jill moved on. The next window was the room where the younger children played. I was determined to keep going, but in spite of my resolve, I stopped when I saw a flash of a blond-haired boy. I do mean a flash, because he was going super speed down a twirling slide onto a floor covered with plastic balls. He looked about five. He had the most delighted grin on his face as he threw balls up and bounced around. I caught his green eyes and immediately an image of Max came to my mind. *He would have so much fun in there,* I thought, and sighed.

"C'mon, Robin, we'll miss the beginning of the class." Jill gave me a queer look as I hurried up. Even though Jill knew about Max, she didn't realize how much I thought about him outside of the park. I hadn't said anything to her recently about Max, and didn't need advice or questions. I didn't know why I thought of him. After all, it wasn't as if it were all the time or anything. I only thought of him when something reminded me of Max. I even have learned to keep thoughts of him away in the back of my mind. A neatly wrapped package, brought out only at a convenient time. I assured myself that this was one of those times. Unfortunately, I also knew from experience that if I did manage to suppress my thoughts of him for too long, he'd come back to haunt my dreams.


Over dinner, I told David about the sumptuous deserts we learned to make at the culinary class. Earlier in the cabin, David showed me the lovely set of golf clubs he won at the contest. It was a very rewarding day. We were looking forward to Jamaica.

Jamaica was such a whirlwind of events. We tried rafting and snorkeling at the reefs. David and Tyler got in some tennis while Jill and I hit the shops. The Calypso show in the evening was wonderful. I loved the reggae music and watching the dancers. Calypso movements look so free and happy.

At the Calypso show, one of the dancers pulled me out of the audience. He put his hands on my hips to help me sway more smoothly. I was uncomfortable. Jill and Tyler laughed and clapped for me. I glanced at David, he smiled a tight smile. I could see the tenseness in his eyes and face. I did a quick dance then went back to my seat. David's arm came around me possessively. I snuggled into him and his grip relaxed.

We sailed toward the Grand Cayman Island. The captain had told us about the stingrays that eat out of your hand when you go snorkeling. I couldn't wait to see them.

That night, David and I spent some time alone in our cabin. I expected this after my dance with the Jamaican. David would never admit it, but it bothered him that some other man touched me, even in such a casual way. I knew it upset him and tonight he needed my reassurance that I was solely his to touch. That only his hands could caress me in ways that could bring us both to the brink of ecstasy.

Afterward, we both lay in each other's arms. David's head was cushioned on one breast while he softly toyed with the other one.

"Don't start what you may be too tired to finish," I teased. He didn't look up, but I could feel how tense he was.

"You're mine, Robin," he spoke quietly, into my breast. I could hear the anxiety in his voice. I kissed his soft blond hair.

"Only yours, David." He sighed as the tenseness completely flowed from his body, satisfied by my assurances. Then he picked up his head and looked at me with a devilish grin.

"I always finish what I start."

The Grand Cayman Island took my breath away. I took so many deep breaths of the fresh sea air that Jill warned me not to hyperventilate.

"I'm storing it up for New York," I retorted.

"Well in that case." Then Jill proceeded to also breathe deeply. We all laughed.

The snorkeling was fun. The feel of the stingray as it softly nuzzled my hand for food was incredible. It sent shivers up and down my spine. Jill and I sunbathed while the boys jet skied some more. David even tried water-skiing, which he managed, no surprise very well.

There was a huge barbecue, for dinner. A multitude of various seafoods and meats were grilled. There were also luscious Caribbean fruits and the Jamaican dish ackee and saltfish. This was made from the fleshy lobes of the seeds of the ackee tree, and cooked with tomatoes, onions, and pepper in oil. I had tried it in Jamaica. I also sampled naseberries, star apples, plaintains and boiled green bananas. David looked at my plate when I returned to the table.

"Well, you're sure adventurous. I just hope you don't get sick eating all those strange things," he added with a glare. Jill had sat down at the same time as me.

"Don't listen to him, Robin, you should try what you want." David glanced at Jill's plate and smirked. It looked as varied as mine.

"Tyler, you and I will have the day to ourselves tomorrow as the women recuperate." Tyler laughed. David always stuck to foods that he was familiar with.

The sun began to set as we finished our meals. We sat and basked in its glow, as we drank Tia Maria liqueur, a coffee, and rum blend. As the darkness descended, we made our way back to the ship. Jill was ready for dancing. I was tired and thankfully, David was too. We said goodnight and went back to our cabin.

Too soon, we were in Cozumel, Mexico, the last stop on our cruise. Jill and Tyler wanted to go horseback riding. David hates horses, so I suggested a tour of the Mayan ruins. I was interested in anthropology as David knew. He reluctantly agreed, since he had already done all the things he wanted to do at the other places we had been to.

After a brief video shown in the ship's movie theater on the lives of the Mayans, we went ashore to see the ruins. It was fascinating to see the actual dwellings. I tried to put the people I saw in the video in the homes that we were seeing now. In my mind's eye, I reconstructed their clay structures and pictured their daily lives. I listened intently to the tour guide until I heard David sigh with boredom. I turned to him and saw his eyes had that glazed-over look, as he stood leaning against a wooden pillar. I walked over to him and whispered,"Do you want to leave?" David straightened up,

"What? Sure!" As an afterthought he added, "Only if you want to?" He looked at me hopefully. I sighed and gave a small smile.

"Sure, I've heard enough."

"Okay, let's go." David smiled and took my hand. I reluctantly followed trying to hear the last words of the guide.

David would have stayed if I had asked him. But I would have had to listen to him tell Jill and Tyler how boring it was. This would have ruined it for me. This way, by leaving, he wouldn't.

Back in Cozumel, we did some window-shopping. I noticed that David was slowly losing that relaxed feeling. He had started to think about returning to work.

Work was David's vacation. He enjoyed the continuousness of his job. His world revolved around order and control. Work was a very safe place for David. Going on trips was very difficult. New worlds and meeting new people was tough, it stressed him.

David pushed himself to take these elaborate trips because it made him feel worldly, he thought. I admit I was glad he felt he had to travel, because I loved those trips. I hugged his arm. He smiled down at me.

"Penny for your thoughts," I said. He laughed,

"They're worth more than a penny. I was thinking of the new account Stuart wants me to start on when I get back. He e-mailed me last night with some information and said..."

I let him drone on about it. I put in the necessary "really" and "that's great" where appropriate. Poor thing, David really had no one to talk to that past week about work. Tyler lived in the plant world, and Jill and I weren't much help.

We stopped for lunch at an outside café. It was cute watching all the sombreros and Mexican blankets carried or worn by the tourists as they walked by. I saw a little boy holding an adorable Mexican marionette. "Max would love that," I thought. I could picture Max laughing at the puppet and I knew I had to buy him one. I told David. After lunch, we went to a shop and found the perfect one. I had the man wrap it in a box for me and put a bow on it.

"You're going to a lot of trouble with this, Robin. Max will like it if you just hand it to him. By the way you have described the Johnsons, it sounds like he doesn't get many gifts anyway."

"That's the point, David, I like to make the things Max does get from me special."

"Okay, fine," David said in a 'let's get going' voice. I hurriedly paid the man and we headed back to the ship. David thought my whole friendship with Max was strange, but he had decided that as long as I didn't talk about him too much, he could tolerate it.


The grand ballroom was redecorated in a glorious tribute to the Caribbean islands, for the end of the cruise party. The buffet was endless and the champagne flowed from ten different fountains. Waiters were hustling back and forth from the kitchen. The musicians played every type of music imaginable. There were two ice sculptures, one of a school of dolphins suspended in mid-air, the other, a beautiful replica of our ship.

David and I danced a couple of waltzes. Later, Jill and I joined the conga line, and Tyler joined David at the table. When we finally sat down, we found them both conversing with the captain. The night before, we had had dinner at the captain's table and the three of them got on very well. Actually, the captain wanted to refer some business to the bank and they were discussing details.

We left the ballroom early that morning. I was exhausted and David sweetly carried me into the cabin and lay me on the bed.

"Whoa," he said straightening up, "another few days at sea and I won't be able to lift you anymore."

I threw a shoe at him. He dodged the shoe, laughing, then plopped down next to me.

"There's nothing like a vacation that allows you to come home bringing the boss some extra work." He was very proud of himself. I rolled over to him and kissed his soft lips.

"You are a brilliant negotiator. Stuart will be thrilled." David kissed me deeply. He intended to say something, changed his mind, and kissed me again.

Early the next morning, the four of us made our way, bleary-eyed, down to breakfast. I watched the porters unload the luggage and put it on the shuttle that would take us back to the airport. We hesitated, not wanting the trip to end, but finally made our way down the gangway. The captain shook hands with David and told him he would be in touch. We settled ourselves in the shuttle. I mentally began to prepare myself for the return to New York and the northern cold.

In spite of my fears, Manhattan greeted us at sixty degrees. As soon as I dropped my bag in the apartment, I went to my greenhouse to see my plants. Bill, who was bringing up the rest of the luggage, assured me as I opened the patio door.

"Your cleaning woman checked on them every day, Mrs. Pierson." I waved at him not to worry, but wanted to see them for myself. I came back as David was locking the door.

"Everyone seems to be well and accounted for," I said.

"What a relief!" David said sarcastically. "Now I'll be able to sleep tonight."

"Funny," I replied. David brought the bags into the bedroom. I followed him and readied dirty clothes for the laundry. He stopped me and hugged me, clothes and all.

"I'm not ready for this vacation to end yet, Robbie. I know a Jacuzzi that feels a lot like the whirlpool on the ship," he said, holding me close. We pretended we were still out to sea, and that the temperature was not steadily dropping.

# Chapter 14

It was a cold February day. I walked toward Central Park hoping that Max would be there. I held a boy's winter jacket for him.

I had seen Max only once since I had got back from the cruise. It was at the end of January. I had brought him the marionette that I got him on my trip. It was a cold day and I wasn't even sure Max would be at the park. He was there, but he only had on the same thin windbreaker.

Max's cheeks were rosy with cold and when I touched his hands, they were freezing. Mrs. Johnson was ready to leave the park for the day. I wanted to say something, but, instead, I just gave Max a hug and the marionette. I watched until Max was out of sight, then I turned, left the park, and shopped. It took my mind off Max. That's when the idea of the coat came to me. I didn't want to have to explain the coat to David, so I decided to wait until the next time I was going to the park and buy it then.

I had gotten up early, and bought a boy's winter coat. Now I was trying to think of a way I could give it to Max without offending the Johnsons.

I was worried about him. He did seem happy, though, while he played on the playground. The Johnsons had warm coats on the last times I saw them. I was angry at them for not dressing Max properly. *I should report them to child welfare,* I thought angrily. "Don't get involved," I heard my mother's words repeat themselves in my head. I thought of David and knew I wouldn't report anything. What if child welfare wanted my home number? They could call me and David could answer. After all, Max was just a little boy that I spoke with at the park. I knew if I got more involved, David might not let me see Max at the park anymore.

I wasn't sure why I had such an attraction to Max, but I couldn't deny it to myself anymore.

I walked into the park gripping the jacket. I would just have to satisfy myself by giving Max some of the things he needs. I was worried. What if the Johnsons got insulted by my giving Max the jacket? They were okay about the trucks I gave him for Christmas. That was a toy, though, clothes are different, personal.

I decided to tell the Johnsons that my friend gave me the coat after her little boy outgrew it and wanted to know if I knew any boys that would fit into it. I would tell them that Max is the only little boy I knew that is this size. They should be okay with that. Feeling better, I headed toward the playground.

The Johnsons were sitting on their bench in their warm coats drinking coffee. Max was still in the windbreaker. I clenched my teeth and commanded myself to be nice. I walked casually over. Max saw me and ran over, calling my name.

"Hello," Mrs. Johnson said, smiling. "Nice day, ain't it." Mr. Johnson just grunted as Max launched himself at me in a grinning bear hug. I hugged him back as Mr. Johnson glared at us.

"What that?" Max asked pointing at the coat.

"Oh, uh, Mrs. Johnson if you don't mind, I brought this for Max." Mrs. Johnson raised her eyebrows in surprise.

"He's warm enough, that coat he got on is plenty warm." Her friendly voice was turning cold. I knew getting into a battle with the Johnsons would not get Max this coat.

"I'm sure it is," I said sweetly. "My friend gave me this coat. Her little boy is too big for it now and she didn't know what to do with it. I'm not sure what to do with it either. I really wish you could help me out by taking it." Mrs. Johnson stared at the coat. I looked at it, seeing it through her eyes. I had purposely bought something inexpensive, but I mentally kicked myself for not rubbing some dirt on the sleeves. The coat looked brand new. I smiled weakly.

"My friend's little boy was very neat," I added.

Mrs. Johnson harrumphed but said, "Well, I guess it's alright, wouldn't want it to go to waste." I helped Max put it on as he jumped up and down. I zipped it up and it was a perfect fit. Max's eyes shined brightly as he fingered the warm nylon.

"Max!" Mrs. Johnson yelled. "Where are your manners, boy? Can't you thank Miss Robin?" I tried to say it was okay, but Max didn't mind being yelled at. *I'm sure he's used to it,* I thought ruefully.

"Thanks, Robin," he said grinning "Come play." Max took my hand and led me away. I looked over my shoulder and saw Mrs. Johnson take out a magazine as Mr. Johnson started snoring. I breathed a sigh of relief, thankful that the ruse worked.

I pushed Max on the swings for a while and then watched him climb the monkey bars. I was about to leave him when I heard yelling from Mrs. Johnson's bench. I hurriedly helped Max down and we ran over to them. A few people were watching, I pushed through them and froze. Mr. Johnson was lying on the grass, not moving. Mrs. Johnson hovered over him crying and calling his name. Someone had called for an ambulance. I heard the sirens as they approached.

"What wrong, Robin?" Max was holding on to my leg.

I picked him up and said, "I'm not sure, Max. Mrs. Johnson was beside herself. I tried to reassure her as we saw the paramedics come over. They carried a stretcher. Mrs. Johnson followed the paramedics and climbed into the ambulance, still crying. She seemed to forget all about Max. Max stared after her, petrified. He thought he was being left. I pushed my way through the crowd, still holding Max.

I quickly explained who Max and I were to the police officer. He told us to get in his car. We followed the ambulance. Max was quiet but he clutched me tightly. *I'll just stay at the hospital until Mrs. Johnson has a chance to calm down and Mr. Johnson's okay,* I told myself. I held Max closely and tried not to think anymore.

I carried Max into the emergency waiting room. A nurse talked to Mrs. Johnson. Mrs. Johnson seemed calmer. I walked over as the nurse left. I sat down with Max on my lap.

"Mrs. Johnson?" I said quietly.

"That nurse is going to call my daughter."

"What happened to Mr. Johnson?"

"Them doctors don't know yet, they think he had a heart attack." She still didn't say anything about Max.

"Mrs. Johnson, do you want me to take Max to get a snack or something?" She looked at Max as if seeing him for the first time.

"Yeah, sure, go on." Then she said, as an afterthought, "You be good, Max."


Max held my hand as we tried to locate the cafeteria. Max was still quiet, not upset, just overwhelmed. We found the cafeteria and I bought him some cookies and milk. The cafeteria workers made a fuss over him and gave him a little stuffed teddy bear. Max perked up and enjoyed his snack.

The cafeteria workers directed me toward a children's waiting area. There was a huge train set. Max took off for it immediately. I sat down and glanced at my watch. I couldn't believe it was only eleven a.m. I felt like it had been a week since I walked to the park holding the jacket. I let Max play for a while, then I guessed I should find out what was going on.

My heart gave a lurch when we returned to the emergency waiting area. Mrs. Johnson was being held by a woman who I assumed was her daughter Mildred. Mrs. Johnson was sobbing as if her heart was broken. I hurried in. The daughter glanced up and glared at Max.

"I told you not to take that boy, Mama, it was too much for you and Daddy. Did you listen to me? No! Now look what's happened. That boy wore Daddy out, that's what he did." I covered Max's ears with my hands. Max just stared at the floor. I'm sure my face, showed the anger I was feeling, but I couldn't control it.

"Excuse me," I said, somewhat nastily.

"Who the hell are you?" the daughter answered, just as nasty. I took a deep breath and tried to calm my voice. Yelling would only upset Max more.

"I'm a friend of Max's." The daughter started in surprise. She was going to say something when Mrs. Johnson interrupted.

"It's okay , Mildred. She's a nice lady, that's all." Mildred's harrumph reminded me of her father. I asked about Mr. Johnson, and this set Mrs. Johnson to wailing again.

"My father's dead," Mildred said stonily. I stared down at Max, who gazed up at me with eyes that were too old for a four-year-old. I wanted to ask Mildred more but didn't dare with Max listening.

Thankfully, a caring nurse came over. She asked Max if he would like to find a friend for his teddy bear. Max nodded yes and took the nurse's hand.

I sat down not knowing what to say. Mrs. Johnson continued to cry, as Mildred held her.

"It's alright, Mama, I'll handle everything and after the funeral, you'll come live with me," Mildred said.

"What about Max?" I asked. Mildred turned fierce eyes towards me.

"You think I'll let that kid wear out my mama too? I'm gonna go call his social worker, Mz. Stacey, and get her to come pick up Max. I should give her a piece of my mind giving wild boys to older folks, what was she thinking?" Mildred untangled herself from her mother and went to the pay phone. I sat quietly not knowing what to say. Mrs. Johnson calmed down a little.

"You have to forgive Mildred, she's just in shock. I guess we both are. She don't mean what she said about Max. They just never got along too well. Max is really a good boy."

"Good , Mrs. Johnson. I knew you would keep him."

"Oh, no I can't. I 'm gonna go live with Mildred. I can't take care of Max myself. Why don't you take him, Miss. Robin?"

I froze. David flashed through my mind.

"I'll just tell Mz. Stacey," Mrs. Johnson continued, "how good you is with Max." I said nothing.

Mrs. Johnson and I sat quietly together, both lost in our own thoughts. Mildred came back just as the nurse reappeared holding Max's hand, his other was filled with two teddy bears and some candy.

"Well, that's done," Mildred said, walking toward us and wiping her hands on her skirt as if Max was some sort of dirt to wipe away. "Mz. Stacey will be right over. Come, Mama, let's go get you some coffee and then take you home." Mrs. Johnson turned to say something to Max, but Mildred tugged on her arm.

"Let's go, Mama, the nurses will take care of the boy till Mz. Stacey comes." Mrs. Johnson was confused enough that she let Mildred meekly take her to the cafeteria without another backward glance. I stared at their retreating backs. I would have felt sorry for Mrs. Johnson. She seemed so lost now, without Mr. Johnson. However, I was too worried about Max. I turned and looked at Max. He face showed confusion and fear. His whole familiar world had just crumbled around him. I went to him and knelt down, lightly taking hold of his shoulders.

"It's okay, Maxie, Robin's here." He slowly turned his gaze away from the retreating Mrs. Johnson and focused on me. His hazel eyes were full of unanswered questions. He smiled weakly and put his head on my shoulder. I made no promises for what the future held. I hugged him and comforted him for the present.

Mrs. Stacey arrived at noon. Max and I had waited for her in the children's area. She walked over to me and sat down.

"You must be Robin. I'm Jean Stacey." I was puzzled that she knew my name, she smiled at me and continued.

"I saw the Johnsons as they were leaving," she  explained. ""Mrs. Johnson thought you might be still here. She tried to apologize for her hasty departure, and to assure me she hadn't abandoned Max. Mrs. Johnson said you were a good friend to Max and would make a great foster parent." My eyes widened at this, but Jean continued. "The daughter told her not to think of Max anymore and took her home." Mrs. Stacey sighed. "Is Max alright?" She looked doubtful. I was not going to assure her that Max was fine just to make her feel better. I was angry with her (and maybe myself?) for leaving Max in a home where nobody seemed to care about him. I guess my feelings showed on my face, because Jean looked at the floor as if embarrassed.

"The Johnsons are not our choice for parents of the year," she said, "but they aren't bad people either." She looked at me as if willing me to understand. "I know they weren't affectionate with him, but they cared for him in their own way. When he was first brought to the Johnsons, he was an infant. Mrs. Johnson fussed over him and was thrilled to have him, then. She said she always wanted a baby boy. She would show me the outfits she bought for him and the toys and they seemed like the perfect foster parents.

"My supervisor was concerned about their age, but I assured him that they were stable. Mr. Johnson had a good job and we were short on foster homes. The daughter was never happy about the arrangement, but she and her husband lived in Queens and they weren't around much.

"When Max was two, Mr. Johnson hurt his leg and had to go on disability. He wanted Mrs. Johnson to give Max up, but she was fond of him. She told her husband they could use the extra money from foster care. I began to get concerned when I would visit and Max was wearing worn out clothes in too small sizes. Mrs. Johnson would assure me that they were just a little short on cash for clothes; but that they were expecting some money soon and would buy Max some new outfits. At that time, we were really short of good foster homes, and Max seemed content. He even called Mrs. Johnson 'Mama'. I felt it would be detrimental to Max's sense of well-being to remove him."

I tried to take this all in as I watched Max playing with the train set.

"Surely you saw his care was getting worse as he got older?" I said.

"That was just it. I didn't make the connection until later. As Max grew older, Mrs. Johnson seemed to care for him less and less. It was the infant Max not the child Max that Mrs. Johnson was so enthralled with. I also noticed that Max was calling them Mr. and Mrs. Johnson, which I thought a little strange. Nevertheless, he seemed happy and didn't show any signs of abuse. I think the reason they kept him was that they needed the money, but were too ashamed to admit this. My agency is bombarded with abuse calls, and we needed to find homes for these children. Compared to what I see, Max had it pretty good." I sighed.

"When I would talk to Max alone, as he got older, he told me Mrs. Johnson would read him stories and sometimes she would bake cakes with him. Therefore, I left him there. I rationalized that it was the only home he knew, and I didn't want to break up the one stable thing in his life."

"Where are his parents in all this?" I asked.

"His mother died in childbirth and his father is not known. He was almost adopted a couple of times, but some complication on the part of the adopting families came up, and obviously both adoptions didn't happen. It takes a lot of time for the adoption process to finish and so by the time the second one fell through, Max was almost four. Four-year-olds are not as easy to place. I thought the Johnsons might have adopted him themselves, but then the accident to Mr. Johnson happened and....." Jean sighed and looked at Max.

I sighed as well. I looked out the window, trying to absorb all this information. Jean jolted me with her next comment.

"What about you, Robin? How do you fit into this picture?" I proceeded to explain my relationship with Max. I began at the beginning, but was brief.

"Let me get this straight. Your husband is vice-president of a bank and you stay home. Max knows you and obviously feels comfortable with you. Mrs. Johnson thinks highly of you. A few background checks and a speed up of paperwork and we may have a happy ending here after all." I cleared my throat a couple of times. I didn't know how to explain David,

"I'm not sure. I mean I don't think, it's just that..."

"Robin, what is it?"

Tears came to my eyes and I choked on the words. I tried to think of a way to explain my world without making David out to be some kind of unfeeling monster. How could I possibly bring Max home when I couldn't even have a real dog? Jean continued to look at me.

"I can't," I began lamely. "My lifestyle, it just wouldn't work out. I'm so sorry."

"Don't be," she said smiling, "I shouldn't have put you on the spot like that. It's a rare person that can open their homes to a child that's not their own. Why do you think we have a shortage of good foster homes? I'll take Max for the weekend and I'll have a place for him Monday."

"Can I still visit him?" I asked tentatively.

"Of course! Everyone needs a good friend." I wasn't sure how good a friend I was but I smiled at the comment.

Max came over.

"Hi, Mz. Stacey! What you doing here?" Jean gave Max a hug.

"I've come to see you!"

"Where's Mz. Johnson?" Max looked around as if suddenly sensing something wasn't right.

"You know, Max, I'm really hungry can we go get some lunch?" Max smiled at this.

"You coming, Robin?" he asked, and grabbed my hand.

"Definitely." I squeezed his hand and we all walked to the cafeteria.

After lunch, we sat outside, Jean tried to explain what was going on to Max. Max sat on my lap and Jean held his hand.

"Mz. Johnson don't want me no more?" Max's lip trembled. I hugged him.

"No, Max, it's just that she is going to live with Mildred. Mildred has a really small house. So Mrs. Johnson can't take care of you like she did," Jean said. We weren't sure if Max understood what happened to Mr. Johnson, but since he didn't ask, we didn't want to go into too much detail.

"You are going to stay with me over the weekend, won't that be fun? And then I know a wonderful family that would love to have a little boy like you." Max gripped my hand and looked at me.

He said in a teary voice, "Maybe I go live with you, Robin?" I choked. I tried to reply but no words would come out. Jean jumped in.

"Max, I really want you to stay with me. We'll have a wonderful time, and Robin doesn't live in a house where she can keep a little boy."

"Could I just bisit you, Robin, till I go to a new house. I won't live there, I just bisit," Max said this with finality. As if he would deal with a new family if he could just have me for a little while. I blinked hard. Not sure whether to laugh or cry at the way he pronounced 'visit'. His courage was unbelievable, and his faith that I would get him through this twisted my heart, as if I was being tortured.

"Max," Jean began softly, but I interrupted her. I felt my own courage awakening and pushing my fear away.

Thoughts of David flew away as I said softly, but succinctly, "I'll take you Max, until Mrs. Stacey's new family will be ready."

"Robin," Jean whispered so Max couldn't hear. He was hugging me so hard I didn't think he paid her any attention anyway. "You don't have to do this, I can take Max."

"I'm doing this. I can do this much for Max."

"Do you need to discuss this with your husband first?"

*Why?* I thought. *He will just yell and say absolutely not!*

"No, it's okay. I'm sure it will be fine," I said in a voice I didn't recognize as my own.

"Okay," Jean said, not sure that it was okay at all. "Just for the weekend. I really shouldn't do this," Jean said, twisting her hair and looking worried. She looked at Max, whose face was pressed into my neck. She reached out and softly rubbed his back. "I don't think I could pry him from around your neck anyway," she said smiling. I smiled back weakly.

"Come, I'll drive you to the welfare office. You'll need to be fingerprinted and a background check done on you. It will only take a couple of hours."

# Chapter 15

Jean drove me and Max to my apartment. She came upstairs to do a cursory check of my home. She asked when David would be home, so she could speak with him. I told her that he worked very late on Friday nights and that he knew about Max and would be fine with this arrangement, being that it was only for the weekend. I winced inwardly as I said it, I had never been good at lying. At least part of it was true. David did know who Max was.

Jean then assured me that the family, I think they were called the Westons, would take Max on Monday. Jean left, saying that she'd call tomorrow. I smiled at her in what I hope was a reassuring manner.

I introduced Max to Bill the doorman, then we went back upstairs. The day seemed to have caught up with Max. I sat him down on the sofa. He looked so small, surrounded by white leather. He sat, and stared at his torn sneakers. His hair fell softly on his face, hiding a bewildered look. I glimpsed smudges of dirt from the park, or maybe yesterday, I couldn't tell. *Why didn't I think to wash his face at the hospital?* I asked myself. I sat down next to Max and pulled him onto my lap.

"This has been a long morning huh, Max?" I crooned a nameless but soothing tune under my breath. I swayed gently as I held him. He held himself rigid except for his head, which he laid on my shoulder. Soon, his body relaxed. We sat like this for some time.

Max said, interrupting my song, "Robin?"

"Yes Max?" I said, gently caressing his hair.

"Mz. Stacey say Mz.. Johnson don't want me anymore, right?" It was the last thing I thought he'd say, I hesitated, not sure what he wanted to hear. The idea of being unwanted was upsetting him. I knew he needed to know that whatever happened next, he knew he was wanted by the people he looked to as his "parents".

"Of course Mrs. Johnson wanted you, Maxie. Don't you remember what Miss Stacey said? That with Mr. Johnson gone, she can't give the proper care you need. You need to be with someone who can take care of you the way a little boy needs to be taken care of. Miss Stacy said the Westons are going to love to have a sweet boy like you." Max didn't answer for a moment.

Then he said so softly that I needed to bend my ear toward his mouth to hear him, "I wish I could stay here."

"You are going to stay for the weekend," I said quietly.

"I wish I could stay forever," he answered me. *Oh Max,* I thought, *I want you to stay with me forever, but I'm not even sure David will let you stay for the weekend.* I brushed that chilling thought from my mind and in my usual way, shut all the things I didn't want to deal with away.

It was almost four-thirty. I knew David would not be home until at least eight. He always went out for drinks on Friday night with Stuart and Ben. I turned Max toward me so I could see his face.

"Listen, Max, let's pretend that you're my little boy for the weekend and you came here to just play and play."

"Okay!" said Max his face brightening at the idea.

"Let's go wash you up a little and then we'll go get a special dinner." Max hopped off my lap. I took his hand and we went to the bathroom. My mind refused to look too far ahead.

Max cleaned up beautifully. He ended up taking a bath as we kept noticing new spots that needed to be cleaned. His clothes looked dingier than ever when we went to put them back on. Max didn't seem to mind, but I did.

"Max, let's go shopping !" I said excitedly.

"For what?"

"For you, darling boy!" I said, as I picked him up and swung him around. He laughed as I grabbed my purse and carried him out the door.

We took a cab to a mall nearby. I have only been there a few times and never with David. David hates the crowds and the "type" of people found in a mall. Max and I went from store to store as we bought clothes and toys. Max was in awe of everything.

We ended our "shopping spree" with a burger and fries dinner. I watched him as he ate. Each bite he took was accompanied with sighs of pleasure. I glanced at the packages filled with jeans, sweaters, shirts, underwear, socks, new sneakers, pajamas, and even slippers. Max smiled at me with his mouth full of French fries. *What a sweet boy you are,* I thought, *I wish,* but, I didn't finish the thought, it was too scary.

"Do you like what we bought, Max?" I asked.

"Yes, specially the toys! I never seen so many." Max looked down at the packages of trucks, blocks and stuffed animals to assure himself that they were still there.

"It's getting late, Maxie," I said. "When you're finished, we need to get back to the apartment."

"Robin?" Max said again.

"What Maxie?"

"You're nice to me." I smiled.

"I like you, Max, It's easy to be nice to you."

"I wish."

"What Max?" I said again.

"I wish you could be my mommy. Then I could live with you forever."

"Oh Maxie," I said, not knowing what else to say.

"I know!" Max exclaimed, as if he just had a fabulous idea. "You said we pretend this weekend that I am your little boy, right?" I didn't like where this was going.

"Couldn't I call you Mommy, since I am your little boy? I never called anyone Mommy before." Max sighed and ate another French fry.

"I've never had anyone call me Mommy, Max. I 'd love for you to call me Mommy, for the weekend." Max's head shot up. He smiled at me from ear to ear. *Oh well,* I thought, *what's one more thing that I have no idea how I'll explain to David, I already have too many to worry about one more.*

I looked at my watch. It was almost seven.

"We need to go, Max."

"Okay, Mommy," Max said. He smiled as he took a last sip of soda. I sighed and grabbed the bags.

Max was playing happily in the guestroom. I watched him at the doorway. He was dressed in his new clothes, with his hair brushed back and face freshly washed. He hardly looked like the same child. He turned to me and smiled, his hazel eyes shining.

"Do you want to play with me, Mommy?"

"I'd love to, Maxie, but I need to make dinner for David. Maybe later." Max smiled again and then resumed his play. I watched Max play for another minute. Now that he was all cleaned up, he reminded me of someone, but, exhausted, I couldn't think of who. It hit me like a ton of bricks and a chill ran down my spine. I finally realized why it was this child had so caught my attention, and had not left my thoughts for the past six months. Max looked just like David. I finally admitted to myself how much I cared for Max. He was already a part of my heart. These thoughts bombarded me as I heard the unlocking of the front door. David was home.

I closed the door to the guestroom halfway. Max was so intent on his play that he didn't notice. David looked at the mail. He heard me walk down the hall and glanced up, and then returned to the mail.

"Hi honey," I said, I kissed his cheek. He turned to kiss me.

"Hi yourself, how was..." David's head shot up when he heard a loud screech from the guest room. Max's toy plane must have been coming in for a landing.

"What was that?" David said as he walked quickly down the hall. I grabbed his arm before he got out of reach. He turned and looked at me, eyebrows raised.

"We have a guest," I said simply. The sound of Max's trucks came next.

"A rather noisy guest," David said, still not quite sure what was going on.

"It's Max," I said watching his face. He continued to stare at me, I watched as he went from confused to comprehending to shock.

"Max," he said in a loud whisper, still not believing. "Max from the park?"

"Yes," I answered. Just then I heard my mechanical puppy barking. I had given it to Max to play with too.

"What is he doing here?" The puppy continued to yap.

"David, let's go into the living room and I'll explain everything." He allowed me to lead him to the sofa. He sat staring at me. I told him the whole story beginning to end, about the hospital, even about the shopping trip. He continued to stare at me.

"How could you?" he began in a hoarse whisper, probably not trusting himself to use a normal voice. "How could you invite him here for the weekend without asking me first? This is inexcusable, Robin. I would have never expected this from you." His voice was getting louder as he spoke. I glanced uneasily over my shoulder to make sure Max had not heard him yet.

"David, please, what could I do? He knows me, he trusts me. His whole world was collapsing around him. I couldn't desert him."

"What do you mean desert him? You just said his social worker was there. Let her take him home, that's her job." He was now yelling. I glanced again toward the guest room.

"David, please lower your voice, he will hear you." David took a hard swallow. I quickly tried to calm him. "I know this was a shock to you when you came in, and you're right, I should have called you and told you what was happening. Things just happened so fast that I had to make quick decisions." David interrupted me here.

"And you made the wrong decision, Robin. Well, now you can call his social worker and have him picked up. I will not have him here all weekend. We are not running a babysitting service for needy kids!" David was now yelling louder than before.

"No, David, Max is staying here." Max must have heard the yelling and unfortunately chose this moment to come into the living room. He looked at David. David was looking at me. He was in shock. I have never said no to him before, and he could not believe it. I put my arm around Max.

"What wrong, Mommy?" I heard David suck in his breath. If possible, his eyes got larger than before. I forgot to mention our pretend game to David. That's it, all the cards were on the table. Then surprising me, David grabbed my other arm and raised his hand as if to slap me. Everything was happening so fast. I screamed and Max started to cry. David froze for a second, then roughly let go of my arm. He got off the sofa, grabbed his jacket and keys and left, slamming the door.

I rocked Max in my arms, as we sat huddled together on the sofa. Max was still softly crying. I think he was just releasing all the emotions from an extremely emotional day. I stared blankly at the fireplace. I was feeling frightened and confused. I had seen a side of David that I had thought was there, but didn't really know was there. *No,* I thought. I couldn't believe that David would have actually struck me. Yes, he was angry and he had every right to be. I had altered his world. I thought back to the warnings he had given me. Some subtle, some spoken outright.

I knew his feelings on children, and yet I brought Max home. I paused in my thinking and looked at Max. He had stopped crying and had fallen asleep. I held him closer to me. I had to bring Max home. I had no choice. How could I make David see that?

I stood up slowly and carried Max to the guestroom. I carefully put on his pajamas and put him to bed. He was so tired, he did not stir at all. I tucked his stuffed teddy bear beside him. He subconsciously rolled to it and held it close. He put the thumb of his free hand in his mouth and made quiet slurping noises in his sleep. I brushed back his hair from his face and pulled the comforter closer around him. Then I heard the door slam. I quietly left Max and closed the door to the room.

David was pouring himself a scotch from the bar. I slowly walked to the couch and sat down near the edge, afraid to move. He turned toward me and sat down on the other side of the sofa. He took a swallow of scotch and looked at me.

"You should have told me," he said softly, gruffly.

"I said there wasn't time." I stopped. His hazel eyes stared deep into my eyes. That wasn't what he meant. He meant I should have been telling him all along. Sharing what was going on with Max, on the inside and outside. I looked at him with an incredulous look. Quickly, my mind brought me back to that time months ago when the chickadee got stunned from flying into my greenhouse. How could I possibly share my feelings on Max when I couldn't open my home to a wounded bird? David turned away from me and drew his hand through his hair and exhaled loudly. I stared at the floor. Arguments and panic mixing together. A picture of my mother floated past me. I remembered my mother's advice on the night David and I announced our engagement.

"Let him always be right," she had said, "Don't make waves. Men deserve to make the decisions, they work hard. Your job is to make sure he has a peaceful home to return to at night."

*Oh Mom,* I thought, *that works for you and daddy, and I thought it could work for me. But I want Max.* Then I almost laughed when I thought about what my mother said at Christmas. *I guess I didn't slip this in too subtly, huh Mom.*

My thoughts made me cry. I tried to wipe my tears away without notice. David saw me. He slowly slid over to me and reached for my hand. I couldn't help it, I pulled back. He put his hand under my chin and lifted my face as tears slipped down my cheeks.

I rarely cry and David's eyes reflected his concern fighting with anger. Deep down, I could tell, love was trying to push its way through. I gave a tremulous smile. He sighed and shook his head. His hand left my chin and went to the back of my head, he pulled my face into his shoulder, and softly kissed my ear. The worry, and frustrations of the day finally took their toll.

I fell into him pushing us both onto the carpet. I held David tight and sobbed like a child. The walls that held all my pent up emotions were finally collapsing with the relief that David was still here. David held me. He didn't say anything, just gently played with my hair, which only made me cry harder.

Then as my tears started to lessen and the sobbing quieted, David pulled me from his shoulder, his hands covering my ears. He looked into my eyes. His eyes shining green held hurt and anger, but also fear. I was pushing him out of his orderly world and I could see he was fighting within himself. He gently wiped my face with his hands, as he continued to stare into my scared, bloodshot eyes. I knew his brain was telling him not to budge, not to let this confusion enter his life, but I could see I was pulling his heart toward mine.

I sat silently witnessing this internal battle, praying that his love for me would help him give me this. David broke my gaze and turned away. He took a deep breath, and slowly released it.

"Okay," he said hoarsely. "I guess I can make it through the weekend." I softly screamed and pushed him back on the carpet, hugging him hard. I kissed his face all over.

David laughed, still with strain in his voice, he said, "I want to speak to this social worker tomorrow."

"Yes, David," I said meekly. I was so thankful, I was ready to agree to anything.

# Chapter 16

Sunshine streamed into my bedroom. I felt so disorientated at first I couldn't remember what day it was. I felt tense and didn't know why. Then scenes of yesterday came passing through my brain with a speed that left me somewhat dizzy. I heard sounds in the kitchen. I jumped up thinking Max was wandering around feeling lost. I reached the doorway when I realized it was only David making coffee getting ready to go play tennis. I smiled to myself. His whole world almost came collapsing around him and he was still not deviating from his routine. I turned to go back to bed, *Max must be as worn-out as me,* I thought.

Then I heard a small sound. I looked across the kitchen and saw Max emerging from the guest room. He was rubbing the last sleep from his eyes. David looked up, his back was to me, he watched as Max walked toward him. Max's hand came down from his eyes and looked at David a few feet in front of him. At first, Max froze then he cowered behind his arms and let out a soft whimper.

I started to go to him, but stopped myself when David said softly, "It's okay Max."

Max continued to hide behind his arms, but stopped whimpering. David slowly walked toward him as if moving toward a frightened puppy. He bent down in front of Max and softly brushed his hair with his hand. I felt tears coming to my eyes and blinked them back. Max cautiously lowered one arm enough to peek at David. I knew David had to be smiling at him because he became brave enough to let both his eyes be seen.

"I 'm sorry I scared you yesterday." David was still talking as if to a frightened pup. "My name is David. Would you like some juice?" Max lowered both his hands and gave David a tentative smile while nodding yes to juice.

David stood up and turned toward the kitchen. He saw me standing in the doorway of the bedroom. They looked so cute standing there the two of them. David blushed when he saw me. Max looked at David to see what he was looking at and then also saw me. Max's eyes lighted up as he ran to me.

"Mommy," he screamed. David's smile turned to a grimace and he rubbed the back of his neck hard.

"You know," he said in a somewhat normal voice, "you forgot to tell me how that came about." I blessed him for keeping control. I caught Max as he threw himself at me, and picked him up.

"Oh yeah," I said. "Um, well, um."

"Yes?" David prompted. Then Max helped me out.

"We pretending that she's the mommy and I'm the little boy, right Mommy?"

"Right, Max," I replied. David stared at me and said nothing. Max turned from me and looked innocently at David.

"Do you want to be the daddy?" he asked. David's eyes got round. I quickly said, "Max, let's go see what kind of juice I have." Putting him down and pointing him to the kitchen, I glanced at David.

He must have picked up more than I thought when he watched me meditate, because he was carefully taking deep breaths. I imagined I could hear his mantra, I thought, wistfully, "I will not kill Robin, I will not kill Robin."


David went to play tennis and I took Max to the zoo. It was a little chilly, but warmer than the day before and I put on Max's new jacket.

"I don't need jacket," Max said. I noticed Max had a tendency to drop words out of his sentences. Occasionally regressing back to baby talk. I was sure in his house there wasn't a lot of chances for vocabulary building.

"Max, it's cold outside. Look, I'm wearing a jacket."

"Okay," he agreed reluctantly. I thought ruefully, He's probably right about the jacket. He's so used to going without one, his blood is probably as thick as molasses.

The zoo was busy, with it being both a Saturday and a nice warm winter's day. This was Max's first time here and he was excited.

"Look monkey, look lion," he yelled happily, pointing here and there. I bought one of those throwaway cameras and took pictures of Max in front of the animals he liked.

I liked this zoo because the animals were fenced in with lots of grassy area to roam around on, instead of being kept in cages. I shuddered remembering once when David and I stumbled upon a horrible zoo in North Carolina when we were there visiting friends of David's. The zoo was comprised of sad-looking animals in tiny cages. I was so upset we left immediately after I had complained to the manager. I also wrote letters to the Governor of North Carolina, which probably did nothing, but made me feel better.

David teased me that next I would be out with the protestors when the circus came to town. I replied that maybe I would be, at which horrified that I would make a spectacle of myself, he told me to stick to letter writing, and so I did.

"Mommy,'" Max said, tugging my hand and grinning up at me. "Let's go see that big thing over there."

"That's a rhinoceros, Max," I said taking his hand.

"Rhinoceros," Max said slowly, trying the name out as we walked to the pond where the rhinoceros was kept.

We were sitting and eating lunch at the café in the zoo after seeing most of the animals. After lunch, there was a presentation being done by the zoo staff on bats. I thought we'd check that out and also go to the petting zoo. I looked down at Max happily eating his gorilla grilled cheese and fries. He smiled up at me.

"Are you having fun, Max?"

"Yea," he said simply and went back to eating. I smiled to myself. What was I expecting him to say, that this was the best day ever? I looked down at my fries and laughed at myself for being so naive.

"What funny, Mommy?" I smiled at Max.

"I'm funny, Max."

We finished eating and I tried hard to just think about today and not worry about what tomorrow would bring.

"Hi, Robin, it's Jean, Jean Stacey. How's it going?"

"Well, my husband hasn't thrown us out yet, but he does want to talk to you." She laughed.

"I'm assuming you're being funny."

"It was a shock to him last night. I really didn't handle it well."

"It's hard to handle something like that well, Robin, do you want me to come get Max?" I glanced at Max cheerfully eating toast and jam, and my heart skipped a beat.

"No!" I said a bit too emphatically, "No, no. We're fine. David said Max can stay for the weekend," I said, calmer.

"Let me give you my number and David can call me. I'll be home until five o'clock."

"He'll call you later this afternoon then."

David came home as Max and I were playing with the animal set I bought him at the zoo.

"It sounds like a jungle in here," David said as he walked into the living room. Max was lying on his stomach on the carpet making his lion roar. He looked up and smiled at David, totally forgiving David for yesterday as only a four-year-old can.

"Hi, David, see my aminals." David laughed at the way Max said animals.

"They're great, Max." Max went back to playing and I jumped up and gave David a kiss.

"Jean Stacey, the social worker, called, she wanted to know how things were going."

"Really?" David said sarcastically, "Did you tell her how understanding I was?"

"No, I said there were some issues, I told her you had some concerns and wanted to call her. She said she'll be home until five o'clock. How was your game?" I asked.

"We won. Ben wanted to go to dinner tonight but I told him you weren't feeling well." I tried to look disappointed that we weren't going out but David saw right through it. He gave me a look and went into the kitchen. I followed him in.

"Are you really that upset about not being able to go to dinner. I mean, you can go. They're not expecting me to go being sick and all." I smiled but David glared at me.

"Oh, that would be a nice threesome," David said sarcastically, and then his voice changed to exasperation.

"No, I don't care about not going out. I'm just worried about you, I mean how are you going to be tomorrow, Robin, when the social worker comes to pick Max up. Are you just going to wave and wish him a good life?"

"Well, I um, I haven't thought about that I guess..."

"Of course you haven't thought about that," David said, interrupting me "That's always been your problem. You never think about anything past the moment and I end up cleaning up your mess."

David grabbed the orange juice out of the refrigerator and slammed the door shut. He grabbed a glass out of the cabinet and slammed that shut too. Then he stared at the glass as he poured orange juice in it. Max was ignoring this whole thing and still happily playing with his animals. I was sure he had heard a lot of slamming in his world and the noise was nothing new. I, on the other hand, was standing frozen not sure what to say next. I went to put my arms around David's shoulders and he shrugged me off. I stood staring at the floor.

It took a lot for me to stand up to David yesterday. I wasn't sure I could do it again. I admitted shamefully to myself that the last few days had shaken me. I wasn't sure I could keep up with it all. David turned around and looked at me.

"I'm sorry, David, I know I didn't think this through. It's just, it's just if you could have seen Max at the hospital. He looked so alone and I was the only one he knew and, and..." I quickly wiped away a tear that started to fall, hoping David wouldn't see. I knew I had cried enough yesterday and that he wouldn't appreciate me crying again. He did see, though, and I heard his sigh of displeasure.

132

"No more tears, Robin, tomorrow this Miss Stacey will come and Max will have to go with her, and that will be the end of it, understood?" he said in a whisper that Max couldn't hear.

"Yes, David."

"Look at me," he said. I slowly raised my eyes to his. He was still frowning as he continued, "and there will be no more surprises. I don't ever want to come home and see another dog, cat, bird, child, or whatever that I was not expecting to find, in this house. Do you understand me?"

David's hazel eyes engulfed me and I knew that I was not strong enough to argue this with him. I knew David loved me and when I married him, he made it perfectly clear that I would be cherished, but only if I played by his rules. I was allowed a few challenges to the rules but only if I didn't push it too far.

I looked at Max in the living room, playing with his tiger, and to my eternal shame, I nodded yes, and went to David, needing that reassurance that I was still his. David, seeing that he had won, held me close, kissed me and assured me it would be better this way. I closed my eyes and tried not to think at all.

David went into the bedroom to call Jean Stacy and I went back to Max.

"I hungry, Mommy."

"Let's go into the kitchen and find you something to eat." Max was eating some yogurt when David came back in. Our eyes met, but he said nothing.

"Max," David said. "I just spoke to Miss Stacy and she said she found a family that would love to have a little boy like you come live with them for a while." I turned away quickly and busied myself at the sink.

Max didn't say anything but his spoon stopped midway to his mouth.

"Max, this other family has a house and other kids there for you to play with, and Miss Stacey said they even have a dog. It sounds like a wonderful home."

"I like dogs," Max said quietly.

Max continued eating his yogurt, not saying another word. When he finished, he said quietly, "You bisit me, right, Mommy?"

"Yes, Max, of course I will visit. I know, why don't we go to the pet store and you can pick out something for the dog and then we'll go get some pizza, how's that sound?"

"I like pizza," Max replied. "You come too, David?"

"Sure, Max, I'll come."

"Let me get our jackets," I said, my voice breaking as I quickly left the room. I took a moment to collect myself and could manage a half smile on my return. Max was talking to David about what they should get the dog.

# Chapter 17

Jean picked up Max on Monday morning. I was dressed to go as well. We all went to the Westons home. The Westons lived not far from Central Park, but in a neighborhood that looked seedy. There were children playing in the street and I did see small yards behind the houses.

Mrs. Weston invited us in with a welcoming smile. A baby cried in the background. I saw a girl, who looked to be fourteen, go and pick the baby up. A boy of about sixteen talked on the phone. Two toddlers played on the worn carpet in the living room. There were a few scattered toys about, and I could see the remains of breakfast on the table. Max held tightly to the dog bone we had brought.

Mrs. Weston led us into the kitchen. She stacked the breakfast plates and wiped the table with a cloth. She asked us to be seated, as she poured coffee and placed doughnuts on the table. She told Max to help himself and gave Max some milk. Then she saw the dog bone Max carried.

"Oh, did you bring that for the dog?" Max nodded. Mrs. Weston said, "That was so sweet, Max! Bear is in the yard. Why don't we have our snack and then see him?" Just then, the toddlers toddled in and Mrs. Weston picked them up and gave them bits of doughnut.

"Well, Max, I was very excited to hear about you," Mrs. Weston began. "I think our home can use a big four-year-old boy." Max smiled with his mouth full of doughnut. Mrs. Weston laughed and gave his hand a squeeze.

"Mrs. Weston," I began, But she interrupted.

"Oh, please call me Betty!"

"Okay, Betty, I brought a few things over for Max that we have bought together."

"Oh, that's so sweet. After I introduce Max to Bear, we'll go up to his room."

"Can I see Bear now?" Max said chewing the last of his doughnut. Betty smiled and put the toddlers down, each with a half of doughnut. We walked to the back door, a brown dog lay in the sun. He seemed to be half golden retriever, with his pretty color and size, and must have weighed at least fifty pounds.

"Now don't be afraid, Max. Bear is very friendly," Mrs. Weston assured us. Max walked timidly up with the bone held out in front of him. Bear galloped over and took the bone. He lay down and began to chew it. Max petted him tentatively and then more bravely. He laughed and talked to Bear. We heard a cry come from the kitchen. Betty excused herself. Jean walked over to Max and petted the dog also. I went back to the door. Through the window, I could see Betty talking angrily to the fourteen-year-old girl, while jiggling a toddler to get her to stop crying. I walked inside. Betty turned, when she saw me and smiled, embarrassed.

"A little mishap, but we're fine now, right baby girl?" Betty said to the little one she was holding. The older girl rolled her eyes.

"Robin, this is my daughter Lori." Lori looked sullen. She said a quick hello then left the room." Betty laughed.

"Teenagers, they are a trial." Jean and Max walked back in. Max ran up to me excitedly.

"Robin, Bear likes me, he lick me on my face!"

"Max, let's go see your room now," Betty said.

We followed Betty up the stairs. There was a cot and two cribs in the room, and a dresser and a small table and chair. The walls were painted a soft blue and there were some bright posters of horses and clowns.

"We haven't had time to get a proper bed yet, but we'll get one soon."

"Of course," I mumbled. Max seemed excited about the table and chair. I had never seen the Johnsons' home but I assumed this home was a little more kid friendly. Betty placed Max's things in the dresser and put the toys on the table. Max immediately took his jungle animals out and began to set them up. We walked quietly out and into the hallway.

"I've explained the situation to Betty, Robin, and she understands how you fit into the picture," Jean said quietly. I wasn't sure what was explained, but Mrs. Weston seemed very accommodating.

"Oh, yes, Robin, you can call me anytime you'd like to see Max. Please don't worry about him. He'll be just fine." I peeked back into the bedroom. Max was taking out his dump truck and loading the animals inside. I sighed, but smiled at them both. Jean squeezed my hand.

"I'll say goodbye to Max now, while he's playing."

"Take your time," Jean said. They both walked downstairs and back to the kitchen.

"Max," I said softly as I bent down next to him. He looked up from his dump truck and smiled at me. I hugged him,

"Maxie, I'm going to go with Miss Stacey now. This looks like a really nice home." Max tried to smile but I could tell he was nervous.

"You come bisit me right, Robin?"

"Of course, Max. I know, I'll come back on Saturday. That's only a few days away. I'll come over and take you out for lunch and you can tell me about your fun days here."

"Okay," Max said happily. I gave Max another hug and kiss and left him with his toys.

Jean and Betty had walked back down to the living room. They were each holding a toddler. The older kids were nowhere in sight. I was a little concerned about the older girl's attitude, but Betty seemed to have everything under control. I knew from my brother's kids that teenagers could be difficult.

"I made arrangements to take Max out to lunch on Saturday," I said as I walked into the room.

"That will be fine," Betty said, smiling. "What time should I have him ready?"

"I will be here by eleven-thirty." This way I'd have plenty of time with Max before David gets home from tennis.

Jean drove me home. We talked a little. Jean told me to call her if there was any problem. I left her and went up to my greenhouse. It felt lonely without Max. I tried to assure myself that Max was in a good place. I thought the best thing to do now was to let Max have time to settle in to his new home and for me to get my old life back. I stopped planting to think about when was the last time I had met a friend for lunch or spent the afternoon at the library or museum. I went back to my plants and started planning my week.

David came home early that night. I was surprised to see him as I sorted through the horticulture books I had picked up from the bookstore that afternoon. I came out of the den as I heard David drop the mail on the counter.

"Hi love! What a pleasant surprise," David smiled at me and hugged me close.

"I was thinking about Max and you today, and I was concerned how you might be feeling."

"You are wonderful. I'm fine. The Westons seem like a nice family. Max was happy, especially with the dog." David laughed.

"I am proud of you, Robin. You handled this very well." "I have a surprise for you," David continued. "I just booked our trip to Greece! Two weeks in August in a house right on the beach! That is where you said you wanted to go this summer, right?" David looked at me his face beaming. I felt as if I was getting a treat for both being good, and following directions. David's face had an expectant look, wanting to know that he had pleased me. I smiled and hugged him. David kissed me long and deep, happy that the ordeal with Max was over. I sighed inwardly.

Saturday came swiftly. I tried not to think of Max during the week, though he kept popping into my thoughts. *I just need to know he was okay,* I told myself, *and then I can move on.* I picked up Max at eleven-thirty sharp. I didn't tell David what I was doing today. He said it was fine that I visited Max, but I wasn't sure if he meant this soon. Anyway, he thought Max was out of his life. I didn't even mention his name all week.

Max had a new shirt on, when I picked him up. He looked clean and neat and he smiled at Betty when we left. Betty had assured me that Max had a wonderful week and had adjusted beautifully to his new home.

The taxi that had brought me to the Westons took us to a family style restaurant. Max and I were seated in a booth. The waitress brought Max a kids menu and some crayons to color the menu with. I read the menu to him and he decided on chicken nuggets. He said he had those at the Westons during the week and had liked them. I ordered a salad. I watched Max as he colored. He hummed a little tune while working on his picture. His hair was shiny and the bangs softly fell over his eyes.

"I like your shirt, Max," I said. He smiled.

"Ms. Betty bought it for me." Ms. Betty? That was kind of cute.

"Did you have fun with Ms. Betty?"

"Yeah, she nice, so's Mr. Bob."

*That must be Betty's husband,* I thought.

"I'm glad everyone is nice,"

"Not Tim, he mean."

"Who's Tim?"

"The big boy." He must be the teenage boy I saw on the phone.

"Was he mean to you, Max?"

"No, he yell at Ms. Betty. But then he leave." Maybe, I thought, as most teenagers, he's not home much.

"Is Lori mean too?"

"No, she nice. She don't talk much." I guess no home is perfect. Max seemed happy. Besides, Betty was the one there and Max liked her.

The waitress put down our lunch. Max ate his with gusto as he told me all about his adventures with Bear. He said he loved the sandbox in the backyard. He helps the toddlers dig holes in the sand. He also said Mr. Bob brought him home a sand bucket and shovel. My fears ebbed as I listened to these happy tales.

"Maybe next time you bisit me, we build in my sandbox, okay, Robin?"

"That sounds great Max." I asked Max if he would like to go to the park after lunch. I was unsure myself, worried it might bring back sad memories. Max said that he would like to go the park.

We walked the few blocks to the park. I wondered if he thought about the Johnsons. I guessed it was a four-year-old's way of coping, not talking about things they didn't understand. We had a great time at the park. Then

I brought Max home. I promised Max I would come and see him soon. Betty said to call anytime. I left with a light heart. I would come to see Max again soon. Nevertheless, I also wanted to get back into my groups, my world, the one I had neglected. Celia had called me yesterday and asked for help with a project she had taken on, a restoration of the history museum. Now, I felt I could really be involved again.

## Chapter 18

It had been a week since I had seen Max. I tried hard not to think of him. I had spoken to him once on the phone. He sounded happy. I know I needed to let him move on with his life. I needed to move on with mine. I smiled to myself as I tied the bow to the baby present I picked out for Monica. Jill was hosting a surprise shower and I felt myself getting caught up in the excitement that a new baby always brings.

David left for the club after he gave me a warning not to get any ideas. I sighed. I pictured a tiny baby boy with wisps of blond hair. In my mind's eye, I saw it grow. I tried to see a baby for itself, but it became Max. I sighed again and let go of my images.


"Hi Robin!" Jill greeted me as I entered the room. The ladies of the women's league were sitting on the sofa discussing their gifts. I saw Monica's sister and mother arranging the games and went over to them. She was beaming. This would be her first grandchild.

"Robin, dear! I haven't seen you since the women's league Christmas luncheon. My, how time flies. How are you dear?"

"I'm fine and excited for Monica." Lillie clasped her hands.

Monica's sister, Catherine, added, "I can't believe I'm going to be an aunt! I can't wait until I'm a mother too." Catherine had just married last year.

"Let me enjoy one grandchild at a time." Lillie gave Catherine a hug. "Besides we have to wait until *Saks* restocks their infant department." We laughed.

Jill called out, "Shhh, everyone hide, Monica is here." The girls squeezed themselves behind the sofa. I, with Lillie and Catherine, kneeled behind the wing chairs.

Monica looked confused as she walked in. "Are we having a candlelight lunch, Jill?"

"Surprise!" Monica's face lit up. Her hands fluttered down to rest on her enormous belly. I watched as she softly caressed the baby within, as if she were soothing it from her startled jump.

"Oh my God! Mom! Catherine!" Monica yelped and hugged Jill. We all stepped forward to be greeted. Lillie led Monica to the wing chair decorated for her. Monica knew she was having a boy, so there were blue ribbons all around the chair. She admired the decorations. The day before, Jill and I had hung blue and white crepe paper and huge bows with 'welcome baby' signs scattered around the room. On the coffee table was a floral arrangement with tiny rattles and bottles dispersed within.

"Come on in, everyone. Lunch in the dining room," Jill announced. She had the lunch catered from a Thai restaurant because that was Monica's favorite food.

On the center of the dining room table, there were more blue bows and the cake. Monica took one look and began to cry. Jill came up with the wonderful idea to have the baby's last sonogram picture airbrushed with edible icing, onto the cake. Lillie helped us sneak the picture out of Monica's house. The picture was taken just a few weeks ago , everything was visible. The baby was in the fetal position. The tiny head curled into itself and the legs drawn up towards his body. His tiny feet and miniscule toes peeped out. The picture was painted across the sheet cake with Welcome baby boy Williams written across. Monica and Rob had some definite ideas about the baby's name but hadn't disclosed it yet. Cameras were busy capturing the moment and Monica was again hugging everyone.

After lunch, we played baby shower games and later, Monica opened her gifts. We all exclaimed over the tiny outfits and little baby shoes. I had bought an outfit for the baby and a day of recovery at the spa for Monica. Lillie only brought a few sample outfits. She had furnished the baby's nursery.

I took the bows after each present was opened and made the baby shower bouquet. Jill saw an idea in a book where the expectant mother throws the bouquet just like at a wedding, and the idea being that the woman who caught it would be the next to have a baby.

It was growing late, all the gifts were opened, and the bow bouquet was huge. Monica stood up with help from her mother and sister. I handed her the bouquet and all the women who wanted to participate, stood behind her. I wasn't sure where I wanted to be, so I stepped toward the back of the group of giggling women. Monica tossed the bouquet, hands went up to reach it, but it landed on my chest almost as if it were meant to land there. Lillie came and hugged me.

"I hoped it would be you. It was time you started a family." Everyone clustered around me, and teased. I looked up and caught Jill's eye as she was putting Monica's gifts into a large bag. We stared at each other a moment, a look of concern was in her eyes. I looked away quickly. I felt Jill knew the addition to the family I wanted was not a baby. She said nothing though, and neither did I.

David didn't ask me too much about the shower, probably not wanting to know. I also didn't feel up to volunteering any information. I was happy for Monica, confused for myself. I threw myself into Celia's museum project, trying to forget.

The restoration project took much of my time, weeks had passed, but it was finally finished. I had called Max a couple of times, taking breaks from the project, and made one surprise visit. Betty was not at all happy by that. I apologized. I didn't mean to surprise her, I just wanted to see Max. I played with Max in the Westons' back yard. He seemed okay but a little tense. Betty had said something quickly to him, before we went out to play. Max responded to my questions with tentative answers. I was only there a few minutes before Betty announced they needed to leave. I kissed Max and promised I would come back again soon.

The day after finishing the project, I called the Westons. They were not home, so I left a message. I decided to reward myself with a trip to the park to see the birds. A few should have been back from southern retreats, with spring only two weeks away.

I had on a light sweater and carried a small bag of bread. I walked through the entrance and, feeling happily surprised, saw Max playing on the monkey bars. He hopped down and went to the swings. I looked around for Betty but didn't see her. Instead, I saw Lori, who was sitting on the bench holding the baby. The two toddlers played in the sandbox, nearby. I wasn't sure if Lori would remember me, but I went over to her anyway.

"Hi Lori, I'm Robin, we met at your home when I brought Max over."

"Oh yeah, hi," she said not unpleasantly.

"Where is your mom?" Lori seemed uncomfortable.

"Mom dropped us off and went to run a few errands. She'll be back soon. Besides, I'm fourteen. I know how to look after kids."

"I'm sure you do a wonderful job." She didn't say anything, she placed the sleeping baby in the stroller. Max saw me and came over. There was a cut on his lip and his eyes seemed tired.

"Max, what happened to your lip?" Max was about to say something when Lori interrupted him.

"Oh, he's okay, he fell down in the back yard yesterday." Max looked at her strangely, Lori glared back at him.

"Max, why don't we go feed the birds at our bench over the hill." I said. I felt something strange was going on. I wanted to have Max to myself to find out what that was.

"No. My mom said not to let any of the kids out of my sight!" Lori said, anxiously.

"Your mom knows me, Lori, it's okay if I take Max."

"Mom left me in charge and she'll kill me if anything happens." I didn't want to get Lori in trouble. I wasn't sure what to do. Max looked at me as if he wanted me to do something. The next minute, Betty came into the park.

"Robin! How nice to see you! How have you been?"

"Fine, thanks. I was just about to take Max over the hill to feed the birds. Lori was a little concerned about our being away from her."

"That's my Lori. She is very conscientious when watching the children. Do you want to take him now?"

"Why yes, I'd…"

"Mom." Lori interrupted. "Robin was worried about Max's lip. I told her about how he fell in the yard."

"Oh yes, he was chasing the dog and he tripped, but he was very brave about it."

"But I hurt …." Max tried to say something at this point but Betty interrupted him.

"I know, sweetie, it did hurt a lot. Oh my look at the time! Why we need to get home. Max, I have something special for you in the car." Max forgot what he was about to say in his eagerness to get at his surprise.

"Say good-bye to Robin first Max." Max gave me a hasty hug and they were off. I called out after them.

"I'll call you to set up a day I can take Max."

"Anytime."

I watched as they left. Max was holding Betty's hand and talking as he tried to run to the car. *Well, he seemed happy.* I thought. Surely he wouldn't be running to go home if Betty or Bob were hurting him. Lori suddenly turned one more time and gave me a look I couldn't interpret, but a chill ran down my spine. I shook my head and promised myself I would call tomorrow.

# Chapter 19

I called Betty the next morning. No one answered, I left a message.

I left to go visit Celia. I spoke to her the day before, and she sounded tired. She tried to sound as if it were nothing. I said I would come visit anyway. I taxied over with a care package of muffins and chicken soup.

I was amazed at how pale she looked. Stuart was angry at her for working so hard on the restoration project. I stayed longer than I expected. Celia, insisting she was fine, was trying to complete some work for the women's league. I tried to complete the work for her, without looking like I was taking over. The ploy fell woefully short.

"Robin, I see what you're doing!" Celia said, an edge to her voice.

"Celia, I can do this. You shouldn't be working so hard." Celia rolled her eyes.

"You and my husband are quite the team. I really don't think I'm ready for the rest home yet," she answered shortly. Then she saw the hurt look in my eyes. She squeezed my hand and gave a tiny smile.

"I'm sorry, Robin. I'm not angry at you or Stuart for that matter. Just at my own inadequacies." Celia sighed deeply.

"Celia, please let this work wait."

"You're a good friend, Robin. I think we both did enough for today. Besides it looks like rain." The winds were picking up. The trees in Central Park were beginning to sway. I left Celia to her rest.

I jumped as I closed my front door, and the sound of thunder boomed in my ears. I had just made it home in time. I should have taken a taxi, like Celia wanted me to, I thought, a little angry at myself. I love, the way the air smells before it rains, though. I had no idea the storm would come on so fast. Thankfully, I made it in the building before it began pouring. Bill had the door open as soon as he saw me coming. I laughed, thinking of Bill's comment.

"That was some sprint, Mrs. Pierson. You should try out for the Olympics." I stopped smiling as a bolt of lightning seemed to light up the entire living room.

I hugged my shoulders tightly, as I walked toward the kitchen. The rain pelted against the French doors. The answering machine was blinking. I sat on a barstool, as I pushed the button. I half expected the call to be from David. *He's probably making sure I don't have any windows open,* I thought smiling.

"Hello," a tentative whisper sounded on the machine. I leaned forward anxiously. It was the voice of a young girl. I knew that voice, but at first, a name eluded me.

"Hello, Robin?" I sat bolt upright. It was Lori Weston's voice. The whisper continued.

"Robin, Max needs you, help him. I can't, I tried but…" The receiver clicked and the dial tone buzzed loudly.

I sat frozen with fear. What would make Lori call me and why did she hang up? I jumped for the phone, and called the Westons.

"Hello," Betty answered cheerily.

"Hello, Betty, it's Robin, I'd like to speak to Lori please."

"Lori?" The pleasant voice turned icy. Too late, I thought of what this call might do to Lori.

"Yes, I- I just needed to ask her a question." I couldn't think of a plausible excuse. I have never been good at lying even under the best of circumstances, which this definitely wasn't.

"She isn't here." The ice in Betty's tone was still there. "She took Max out for the afternoon. Why don't you ask me your question." I didn't know what to say. I was afraid to say anything. I didn't want to get Lori in trouble.

"It was nothing. Please just tell Max I called and I'd like to see him next week."

"Of course. We will set up a time. Goodbye." I numbly hung up the receiver. What was I going to do? The storm was getting louder. Then another crash of thunder made me jump off the stool, tumbling it to the

147

floor. Lightning again flashed and the room went dark. The lights quickly came back on again. The answering machine beeped. I turned toward it just as David walked in.

"What a storm! Thank God for parking garages." He hung up his coat and then looked at me for the first time.

"What happened? Please don't tell me you left the windows opened in the den."

"David, something dreadful is happening to Max at the Westons."

"What? What are you talking about?"

"Just listen." I turned to play Lori's message, but it was gone. I then noticed the machine blinking. The message must have been lost when the electricity went off. I said so to David.

"What was the message?" he asked. I explained it was from Lori and what it said. He looked at me with disbelief.

"Are you sure it said help him? Maybe she just wanted to ask you a question about him."

"Then why would she whisper and why would she hang up? Why would she be asking me and not Betty?"

"I don't know," David answered with an edge to his voice. He went to the bar for a drink.

"I called the Westons. I tried to talk to Lori. Betty said she was out. She sounded angry that I asked to speak with Lori."

"Well, that's understandable. Why wouldn't she be angry? You're calling up and asking to speak to their teenage daughter? Christ, Robin, don't you think at all?" I blushed. I already knew how stupid I had acted. I didn't want to hear it again.

"What should I do?"

David took a drink of his scotch.

"I can't believe this kid is back in our lives again," he mumbled, and took another drink before answering. "Call Jean in the morning. Let her take care of it. It's her job, remember?" His tone was clipped. A sure sign that I better change the subject, which I did. I was sure David was right. Jean would take care of this, but why did Lori call me and not Jean?

148

I called Jean in the morning. I first explained the strange meeting in the park and then the phone call.

"Are you sure it was Lori that called?"

"No, I'm not." I had to admit it. "But who else would know Max?"

"That's true. I'll come over and listen to the recording. Maybe I can verify that it's Lori."

"The message is lost," I said sadly. "The storm knocked it out my machine." There was a long pause. My palms became sweaty, I hurriedly added. "Jean, it had to be Lori. Please, Jean, we need to do something."

"I'll go over there today and talk to Lori privately and Max also. We'll see if we can get to the bottom of this."

"Thank you, Jean. Call me as soon as you know anything." I hung up the phone, shaking. I prayed silently for Max and for Lori.

Jean called later that afternoon. I listened, holding my breath.

"Robin, Lori said she never called you and that she would have no reason to call you. She said Max was fine, as well as the other children. Lori also went on to say that you are constantly harassing them and won't let Max adjust to his new family."

"What!" I exploded. "There can be nothing farther from the truth. If anything, I don't get to see Max enough."

"Robin," Jean said softly. "You are not guaranteed visits with Max. If Betty and Bob agree, you can see him. But in no way do you have any legal rights to Max." I sat down trembling.

"Did you speak to Max?" I asked, fighting back tears.

"Yes, he said that he was fine, Robin. I admit he wasn't as relaxed with me as he was when he was with the Johnsons. But this is a new home and he's still adjusting. I also feel that there is some truth to what Lori and Betty are saying. You have to let Max have some time to adjust to his new surroundings, Robin. I think it might be a good idea if you don't see Max for a while, until he's more comfortable with his new home."

I hung up and cried.

# Chapter 20

After a while, I stopped crying and tried to think what to do next. David called as I was thinking, and told me Celia was in the hospital. Stuart was beside himself with worry. He wanted me to go to the hospital to help him. I quickly washed my face and left.

I found Stuart pacing the hallway. At first, they thought Celia had had a heart attack, but it was a panic attack brought on by exhaustion and stress. Stuart blamed himself.

"I should never have let her take on that museum project. She does far too much." He sounded so upset. I tried to soothe him.

"Stuart, you know you couldn't stop Celia. She loves helping others."

"She takes on too much," he repeated. I coaxed him to a chair and brought him some coffee.

I stayed at the hospital for three days, only going home for sleep. Celia said she felt calmer when I was beside her. On the fourth day, she was allowed to go home.

After leaving the hospital, I went home and slept for twenty-four hours. David was angry at me for pushing myself so hard. However, it was Celia, so he wouldn't say much.

I called Betty as soon as I was up, dismissing Jean's warning. I just needed to know Max was okay, but there was no answer. I tried Jean, but she was out of the office. I went to the park. In the playground, I saw Max sitting in the sandbox playing with some sticks and rocks. It reminded me of the first time I saw him with the Johnsons. The older boy was there but I didn't see anyone else. Max didn't seem to hear me when I called him, then he slowly looked up. There was a bruise on his cheek. His eyes narrowed at me. The older boy walked over.

"Can I help you?"

"Hi, I'm a friend of Max's. I was at your house the first day Max came to live with you."

"I'm sorry, I don't remember you. Max, do you know her?" He didn't speak sharply, but I thought I saw Max wince.

"Yeah, she Robin." Max looked at the sand when he said this.

"It's Tim, isn't it?" I asked.

"Yes," he said cautiously. Then he said, "Listen do you have our number? Maybe you should talk to my mother."

"I have your number."

"Why don't you call?" Max cried out, startling me. "You not call in a long time!" Max looked up at me, with eyes full of pain. I bent down to him and tried to explain.

"I'm sorry, Max, my friend was very sick and I had to take care of her. I tried to call this morning but no one was home. How did you get that bruise on your cheek, Max?" Max touched his cheek.

Tim said, "Oh, he got that from the dog, right Max?" Max said nothing, just looked at me. I watched, amazed as his eyes turned the same shade of green as David's. Angrily he yelled, "You said you come bisit me again!" I felt terrible and fought back tears.

"I'm so sorry, Max, but I'll call Miss Betty as soon as I go home. We'll set a day to take you out, how about Saturday?"

Before Max could answer, Tim said,

"We better be going, Max." I hugged Max, but he didn't hug me back.

"Wait, why don't I come too?" Max's eyes lit up.

Tim said, "I think it would better if you called and spoke to my mother." I looked at Max as the light slowly left his eyes.

"I'm coming too, did you walk?"

"Yeah, it's only a few blocks." I left with them. Tim strode ahead, but Max held my hand. I felt his tension drain away.

When we entered the house, we found Lori trying to rock the baby asleep while the toddlers fussed and cried on her legs. Tim went upstairs without another word. I went to Lori and sat down on the floor. I pulled both toddlers on my lap.

"Where's your mom?" Lori didn't look at me, but answered.

"Oh, she'll be right back. She just went to the store for a few things." I looked at Lori, but she continued to focus on the baby, ignoring me. Max sat close to me as I juggled the little ones. I was just about to ask her about the phone call when Betty walked in with a bag of groceries. She screamed at Lori then she saw me.

"Robin! This is quite unexpected."

"I ran into Tim at the park and Max asked me to come over." Betty walked into the kitchen and put down the groceries and came and took the baby from Lori.

"Thank you, Lori, for watching the little ones, you can go to your friend's house now." Lori quickly left, seizing the moment. Betty sat down and rocked the baby.

"Robin, I would really appreciate a phone call before you come over. I don't like the idea of visitors here when I'm not in. Lori and Tim both know that and I think you put them in an awkward spot." Betty didn't say this angrily, but the tone of her voice made Max scoot closer to me.

"I'm sorry, Betty, I tried to call this morning, but no one answered. I understand what you are saying though, and will call next time. How about if we set a date now for me to  take Max out?"

"That will be fine."

"How about Wednesday?"

"Okay, let me have your number though, in case I need to contact you." I gave Betty my number and decided it was best that I leave. I called a taxi, gave Max a big hug good-bye when the taxi arrived and promised I'd see him soon.

When I got home, I called Jean to see if she'd been to see the Westons. I was feeling even more alarmed now about what was going on in that house. Thankfully she was in the office.

"Hi, Robin, I thought I'd be hearing from you again."

"You did?"

"Yes, Betty Weston just called and went on and on about you having dropped by with no advance notice. She said this was the second time you've done that." I almost dropped the phone.

"What? It's not like I purposely planned these surprise visits!"

"That's what she made it sound like. I thought you were going to leave Max alone, so he would have time to adjust?" Jean sounded angry with me. I could not believe I was placed in the wrong. I tried to explain what had happened, but Jean still sounded cold.

"I was there just there, Robin. I didn't see any bruises on anyone. Betty did say Max played with the dog a lot."

"I don't think a dog would leave a bruise like that," I said softly.

"Look, Robin, I have twenty other cases I'm working on. We have never had a problem with the Westons and I don't think there is one now. I don't know how to say this," Jean continued, "but you had a chance to offer Max a home. You couldn't and that's fine, but you can't sit in judgment of every foster home." I didn't know what to say.

"Robin, I'm sorry. It's been a very stressed week. I know you only have Max's best interest at heart, but you've got to let him go, Robin. You have to let him get on with his life."

"I won't go over without calling, but Jean, I have to see Max, Wednesday. At least once more. If only to let him know why I'm not calling or seeing him."

"Fair enough," she answered. I heard her sigh and then we said good-bye. I was shaken from the phone conversation. I wasn't sure if I should say anything to David. I decided not to. He'll probably just say that's what I get for interfering. I was so glad I would be seeing Max the next Wednesday.

# Chapter 21

Wednesday morning showed the promise of a beautiful day. I woke up as David was leaving. I called out good-bye to him. He came back to the bedroom and sat down on the bed beside me. He kissed me softly.

"This is a nice surprise. The last few days you've been sleeping in, you've looked so cute, I didn't want to wake you."

"Yes, well you know I have a tendency to sleep when I'm worried about something."

"What are you worried about?" David asked. I'd forgotten I hadn't said anything to him about Max, except that I was taking him out today.

"Celia, she sounded tired when I spoke to her yesterday." David smiled and kissed my forehead.

"You are a good friend to Celia. Stuart keeps singing your praises. Maybe it's not my expertise in banking after all that gave me that raise last month." David said this, smiling and in a mocking tone. I playfully pushed him off the bed.

"Good-bye David." He laughed and called back as he walked out the door.

"Bye, have fun with Max."

I got up and drank some coffee. It was only eight o'clock, so I went and took a long shower. At nine o'clock, I could wait no longer and called the Westons. I guessed with all the babies, they should all be up. There was no answer. I went to work in my greenhouse. I called back at ten o'clock. Betty answered the phone.

"Hi ,Robin, oh gosh, is today the day you are taking Max?"

"Yes it is."

"Oh dear, Max met a new friend at the park on Tuesday. I just took him over to play at his house. I'm sorry."

"That's okay, I'll take him after lunch." There was a long pause before Betty answered.

"Gosh, he already has plans for the afternoon. Actually, he's busy for the rest of the week. Let's plan another day, how about a week from Friday?"

"Well, I'd like to see him sooner than that." I was beginning to become annoyed, but I knew arguing with Betty would not help me see Max, especially now that Jean seemed to have distanced herself from me as well.

"Let me check my calendar. No, I don't see an earlier date. I started Max in a play program this week at the recreation center. I thought it would be good for him to be around other children his own age. The program meets three times a week."

Taking a deep breath to calm myself, I replied, "Yes, the play program sounds like a good idea. Next Friday will be fine then."

"Thanks, Robin, I knew you'd understand." I hung up the phone.

I thought of calling Jean, but knew that wouldn't help. She would be happy Max was to be with other kids. She wouldn't think anything was wrong and she would be annoyed at me for bothering her. I felt strongly that something was wrong, something was very wrong. Powerless, tears began to well up in my eyes. I went back to bed and cried until I fell asleep.

"Robbie, wake up." I came slowly back to consciousness. David was shaking me. It was dark in the room.

"Are you sick, Robin?" I sat up, still fuzzy. David stared at me, his eyes were full of concern.

"I'm worried about Max." There it was. I had said it.

"You're what?" He couldn't seem to connect my sleeping and my worry over Max.

"I didn't tell you but I ran into him at the park on Monday. He was with his foster brother, and he had a bruise on his cheek."

"Did you find out how he got the bruise?"

"They say the dog caused it somehow. I feel like there is something wrong."

"Did you talk to the Westons and Jean Stacey?"

"Yes, the Westons had excuses for everything. Jean actually got angry at me for upsetting the Westons! Betty cancelled Max today. She said she forgot we had made plans, and that Max was at a friend's house. She says she has put him in a play program next week. I can't see him until next Friday. I think she's lying, David, I just don't have any proof.". David pulled his hand through his hair and mumbled,

"You don't know how I wish you had never met this boy." I looked away from him.

"Listen, Robin, I know you don't want to hear this, but I agree with Jean. When Max was at the Johnsons, you were his friend. You gave him what the Johnsons couldn't or wouldn't. Now he's in a house with kids and more of a family life than he's ever known. Don't you think your problem is you don't want to let go of him? Maybe you still want to be the main person in his life, is that really fair to Max?" I looked down at my hands. I was confused. I didn't know what to think.

I said softly, not looking up, "I don't know, David, I just don't know!" I wiped a stray tear away. David gave me a quick hug.

"Come on, get up and go wash your face. We're going for dinner. I was going to surprise you with this tomorrow night, but I think you need to hear it now. I took Friday off and booked your parents' Christmas gift, a weekend at the Catskills. I definitely think you need a getaway." I hugged David. I told him how thoughtful he was. At the same time, I hoped he was right about Max.

# Chapter 22

I felt refreshed on Monday. We had had a wonderful weekend at the Catskills, and I shared it all with Jill when we met for lunch. Jill had been to the Catskills a few weeks before, so we had plenty to compare, and happily talked the afternoon away.

On Tuesday, I planned to go to the park and stop at the plant store on the way home. I felt relieved that Max was at his play program and I wouldn't see him. I pictured a quiet morning with my birds.

When I arrived at the park, I could not believe my eyes! There was Max! He was playing quietly with the two toddlers while Betty sat rocking the stroller and chatting with a friend. I was livid. I don't think I had ever felt so angry. Betty looked up. She actually grimaced, then quickly pasted on a fake smile.

"Why, Robin! Out enjoying this lovely day?"

"I thought Max was in school this week?"

"He was supposed to be, but they cancelled class today. The teacher was sick. He'll be there tomorrow." She continued smiling. The friend looked at me as if I was slightly deranged. I walked over to Max. I heard Betty whisper, probably explaining me to her friend.

"Hi, Max!" Max didn't answer. I bent down to look at him. He had a new bruise on his forehead.

"Max?"

"What you want?" he said meanly. His eyes were narrowed and a vivid green.

"Max, what is it?"

"You never come bisit, you not my friend."

"Max! I've tried to come. I wanted to take you out a few days ago, but you were at a friend's house. Now you're busy with this new play class."

"Who my friend?" Max replied, and looked as if he had no idea what I was talking about. Shocked, alarms went off in my head.

"Max, dear, we need to go. Take the babies' hands, sweetie," Betty called anxiously. Max stood up and pulled on the toddlers. He walked away, glaring at me. I ran to them as they left.

"Betty!" She was putting the toddlers in the stroller, alongside the baby.

"Yes?" she said.

"Max doesn't know about any new friends or a play class," I whispered harshly.

She then said in a tone that was tired of explaining herself to me, "He's only been there once. I didn't call it a play class to him. I told him he was going to meet some new friends. Max, dear, remember when you met that boy Billy last Thursday?" She continued when Max looked at her in bewilderment. "It was a few days ago, Max, but you'll see all your new friends tomorrow. Robin, I must go now." The friend continued to look at me strangely. I moved aside to let them pass. I tried to hug Max, but he moved away from me.

"At least tell Max I've been trying to come and see him," I said to Betty as she left.

"Why, I always tell him," she said. I was no longer up to going to the plant store, so I went home.

Not knowing what else to do, I waited anxiously for David to get home. Thankfully, he was on time.

"I saw Max at the park today," I said, as I set the table for dinner. David sat on the sofa drinking a martini and looking through the mail.

"Max seemed bewildered today. Worse even than last week when I saw him at the park."

"Robin, I'm sure you're exaggerating." David continued to sift through letters. I put forks and knives by our plates.

"There was another bruise on his forehead," I said, as I stared at the china. "And, when I called his name, he looked at me confused. He didn't want to talk to me. He thought it was my fault that I hadn't tried to visit him."

"Hmm," David replied absently.

"David, are you listening to me?" I said in a voice he had never heard me use before. I didn't realize how upset I was until I heard myself speak. David looked up, my voice had surprised him as well. I hugged my arms tight and looked at him. He put the mail down on the table next to his drink.

"Robbie," he said softly, "I'm sure there's a logical explanation. There is no reason to expect the worst from his foster parents. They seem like nice people. The other kids were clean. Everyone seemed well cared for when you were there. You even admired the dog."

"You didn't see his face today, David. He looked so scared and alone. He actually flinched when I hugged him." My voice began to crack. "There's something wrong, David. I can feel it. The Johnsons definitely could not claim any prizes as foster parents, and yes he's cleaner now. But, oh God, David! You didn't see his face! You didn't see his face!" At that, I put my own face in my hands. I couldn't hold back the tears any longer. David came to me and held me.

"Robin, you have called Jean Stacey. She seems like someone who has had Max's best interest at heart. She said she went back to visit last week and saw nothing wrong."

"I tried to call her again today," I said, between gulps of tears. "The child welfare office said she quit last Friday. She moved to a different state. It had something to do with her husband's job transfer. It was a sudden thing. They gave me Max's new case worker. His name is Steve Andrews. He tried to hurry me off the phone. He made light of my concerns. He said that the Westons have always been rated as a good foster family. He was just there yesterday and he insisted everything looked fine. He said he would check on Max again, but I think he was just saying that to get me off the phone." I started to cry again and I turned away from David, afraid he would get angry with all my tears. David hugged me.

"You said you were taking Max for the day on Friday, right?"

"Yes," I answered, trying to stop the tears.

"If there is a problem with you taking him on Friday, I promise you I will call Betty and this Steve Andrews if need be. You will get your time with Max. Then I know you'll feel better about the whole situation."

"Oh, David, you are the best!" I kissed him all over his face and he laughed.

"I'm sure you have let your imagination run away with you as usual. There is nothing wrong at the Westons."

"I hope you're right."

"I know I am," David said.

I fell asleep that night saying a prayer that David was right. I tried to ignore the persistent nagging thoughts that occupied the corner of my mind. Those thoughts that said this time, David wasn't right.

# Chapter 23

I had woken early after a restless night, knowing I was going to see Max in the morning. I had worked in my greenhouse since eight. I had taken the plants out of the greenhouse and placed them on tables on the patio.

Some of the plants were getting too brown. I brought them back into the greenhouse and exchanged them with others. This was a lot of work, but it helped clear my mind.

When I was done, I walked inside and peeled off my t-shirt and headed toward the shower. I let the cool water run down me, and thought about Max. I couldn't wait to have him to myself. I hadn't spent time alone with him since that day back in March when he had breakfast with me. I finished my shower and called the Westons.

Betty sounded pleasant enough. A child was crying in the background, but I could tell it wasn't Max. I promised myself I would be civil.

"Hi, Betty, this is Robin. How are you?"

"Oh fine, Robin, and yourself?"

"Fine, thank you. When may I pick up Max?"

"Oh, uh, I know I promised, Robin, but Max is sick. A virus. I think he picked it up at his new class. Unfortunately, that happens sometimes. All those new germs, you know." I hated Betty's tone. It told me I knew nothing about children.

"I'd like to come visit him."

"That's not a good idea. He's been sleeping a lot. Actually he's sleeping now."

"How about tomorrow or Sunday?" I asked.

"Oh, um, Sunday we're taking all the kids to Coney Island. Max wanted especially to go, and I told him if he was feeling well, he could. I wouldn't want him to miss out on that. He's been looking forward to it. Another time. Robin, I need to go, the babies are crying. Good-bye."

Betty quickly hung up and I stared at the phone receiver. I couldn't believe she had found another excuse. I sat frozen. I didn't know what to do. Desperate , I did something I never did , I called David at work.

I heard the secretary say, "Hold on, Mrs. Pierson, I'll put you right through."

"Robin, what's wrong, are you hurt?" David's asked.

"David," I said barely, coherent. "Weston said Max was sick, I know he's not. She lied to me! She doesn't want me to see him. Something is wrong. I know it!"

"Slow down, Robin, I can't understand you. You're not hurt? Can this wait until I get home? I'm really swamped here." There was annoyance in his voice.

"David, I'm worried about Max. You said you would help. You promised me, David!"

"Okay, Robin. Give me the name and number of that new case worker. I'll call him and see if we can get to see Max. I'll let you know what happens when I get home."

"Thank you, David."

I sat numb. I called my mother.

"Robin! What is it? Are you okay?" I heard the surprise in her voice. I never called so early in the morning. "Is there something wrong with David?"

"No, we're fine." I could hear my father in the background asking who it was. He called to my mother to help him find his golf shirt.

"Mom, do you remember Max?"

"What dear? Max? Oh yes that orphan." My mother called to my father, "In a minute, dear, Robin is upset. Now, Robin, what about this Max?"

"I think he's being abused at his new foster home. I don't know what to do. David said he would call the case worker."

"Robin! You aren't to bother David. This is ridiculous. He works hard. He doesn't need to be bothered with something that is not his concern."

"He doesn't need to be bothered about the welfare of a little boy?" I shouted at her, incredulously.

"I didn't mean it quite that way. You said yourself he has a caseworker watching out for him."

"The case worker is not watching out for him, that's the point."

"Robin, I realize you want to help, but David must come first. You shouldn't put him in this awkward position. He's busy at the bank. Oh, hold on a minute, dear." I heard my mother placating my father about his golf shirt.

"I need to go, Robin. Remember what I said, people are paid to help this child."

I hung up, and went back into my greenhouse. I watered the plants with my tears.

David came home at exactly six-thirty. I rushed to the door as soon as I heard his key in the lock.

"What did he say, what did the caseworker say?" I asked, as I clenched and unclenched my hands. David hesitated. He hung up his coat, straightened some jackets in the closet and finally turned to me.

"He said, Robin, that he was at the Westons last week and saw nothing wrong with any of the children. He also said that Max plays rough with the dog and that the dog would nip at him. Betty had warned Max about this, but Max loves the dog and Betty has a hard time keeping them apart. Steve said that that was how he got the bruise on his face."

"David, that was a bruise, not a dog bite, I know the difference."

David looked at the mail. He stopped and looked at me.

"Robin, maybe Max tripped and fell when the dog was chasing him. I bet that is exactly what happened." David put down the mail, gave me a quick kiss, and made his way to the liquor cabinet for a drink.

"That doesn't explain why Betty won't let me see Max."

"Well, kids do get sick, Robin," David answered as he poured a scotch and soda. "What's for dinner?"

"Uh. What?"

"Robin," David said sternly. I turned to look at him, surprised by his voice. He was sipping his drink as he watched me.

"Please don't tell me that you are going to obsess about this now." David's voice grew angrier. "I called the caseworker, he said Max was fine, and that's the end of it. I'm tired of Max dominating every conversation we have had lately." David slammed his drink down on the coffee table and sat down on the sofa, roughly opening his journal. I tried to pull myself back together. I looked at David. Resentment burned in me. He said he would help me see Max. One phone call and he was finished.

Part of me wanted to run out of the apartment and straight to Max. I wanted to grab him and keep on running. What would I do without David? How could I leave him. David had always been everything.

*Oh, Max,* I thought, *if there was only more to me, if I was stronger.* Resentment slowly faded, and fear came over me. I was disgusted with myself, but I went to David. I sat next to him. Green eyes glared down at me. I gave him my 'forgive me' look and he smiled.

I lay in David's arms on the sofa. He absently twirled my hair.

"What should I order for dinner?" he asked.

"Whatever you want." I felt safe again, but not happy. Later, I told myself, later, we would talk about Max. I had pushed David too hard. I would go slower the next time.

I knew I needed David. I have always needed David. Now I hated myself for that need.

# Chapter 24

Saturday morning brought a shining sun and a warm April day. I watched as David got ready for tennis.

"What are you going to do this morning?" David asked. I forced a smile.

"Oh, I thought I 'd give Jill a call. I need a manicure and she has a girl she said does a wonderful job." Getting a manicure was the last thing I wanted to do right then, but, I knew this would please David, and it did.

"Great idea. Much better than playing with your plants. Just make sure you're home by two o'clock or I'll be lonely." David kissed my forehead and left. I poured milk in my coffee as I waited for Jill to pick up the phone. On the fourth ring, Jill sleepily answered.

"Hello," Jill said as she yawned into the phone. I looked at the clock; it was ten thirty. I'd forgotten Jill usually sleeps to eleven.

"Robin, you're up early."

"Yeah, well, Jill I need to talk, will you meet me for brunch?"

"Sure I will, when and where?"

"How about the bistro at eleven thirty?"

"I'll be there."

In the shower, I wondered what I would say to Jill. She was my closest friend. The only one who knew the whole story of, Max. She knew more than David. She knew the struggle I was in and the obstacles I was up against. Tyler was not as rigid as David, but there were plenty of issues Jill had to deal with.

I stepped out of the taxi just as I saw Jill walk into the bistro. I hurried to catch up to her. We sat down and the owner walked over to us.

"Mon cherie, Jill! Mon cherie, Robin! What a pleasure to see you both on this bright and sunny day. What can I get for you to drink? A Bloody Mary? How about my special mimosas?"

"That sounds great, Henri," Jill answered.

"Wonderful," I replied. Henri went to get our drinks as a waiter came with menus. We both ordered the chicken crepes. Henri placed our drinks on the table.

"Now," Jill said. "What's up? Trouble in paradise?"

"Jill, I don't know what to do. I'm worried about Max." I took a sip of my drink. Jill stared at me, as she sipped her drink. I continued, shakily.

"I know something is wrong at the Westons." I told Jill everything, a condensed version of what had happened.

"Our husbands do one thing and they call that helping. I'm in shock that David actually called the social worker at all." Jill replied with an ironic look on her face.

"David is trying to help, Jill. It's me, I mean, maybe this is all in my head. Maybe I'm not happy about how I handled the situation with Max."

The waiter placed our crepes on the table. I absently picked up my fork and twirled it in the sauce on my plate.

"Robin," Jill said, "you did everything you could. You helped him when the Johnsons were in the hospital. You brought him home, kept him for the weekend. I'm still not sure how you managed that, knowing David. And, then you made sure he was in a good foster home." I laughed ironically at that. Jill continued. "We must assume it is good, the social workers keep checking it. What else could you do?"

"I could have done more, Jill," I answered. "I still can." Jill took a bite of a crepe and chewed it slowly.

"No, Robin, I'm not sure you can. Our husbands can only be pushed so far. They demand and expect a certain level of consistency in a corporate wife. You know that as well as I do. Disruption is a no-no. As opposite as David and Tyler are, they are plenty alike. Our job is to be there for them at the end of the day when they jump off the roller coaster. In return, we get a lot, but there are also sacrifices to make. It's like being a military wife, except the pay and fringe benefits are better," Jill said, smiling. I smiled back weakly.

"My gosh, they're not ready for their own kids, let alone anyone else's," Jill added. "Take my advice, leave Max in the hands of social services and start praying to the saint of conformity," she said the last with a wink. I turned and looked out the window to collect my thoughts.

I knew part of what Jill said was true. But David has a better place in him that I get just a small glimpse of sometimes, after we make love, or after some tender moment. I know there is more to him than a man on a roller coaster.

Jill startled me by reaching across the table and squeezing my hand. I looked into her eyes. They were full of concern.

"Robin, honey, did I upset you? Did I say too much?" I squeezed her hand back and gave a small smile.

"Jill, you can say anything to me. What kind of friend would I be if I asked for advice and then got angry when you gave it? I'm just upset about Max." I blinked quickly, and looked down at my plate. I did not want to start crying in a public place.

"Robin! Jill! What a surprise!" I looked up to find Joanne holding Bitsy, with a pink ribbon tied around her neck, approach our table.

She sounded like she hadn't seen us for years rather than just last week at the women's club board meeting. Jill immediately engaged Joanne in conversation, to give me time to collect myself.

"Joanne, dear, I didn't know Henri allowed animals in his restaurant?" Jill smiled innocently. Joanne tried to return the smile without grimacing.

"I can see why some people who don't understand breeding in chitzus may think of Bitsy as an animal, but she's really just a little baby. Aren't you, my sweet darling?" Joanne kissed Bitsy. Bitsy obliged by wagging her tail at super sonic speed. "Anyway," continued Joanne, "We're not staying, we just picked up a little something to have in the park while we meet with some of Bitsy's friends at our chitzu club meeting." I breathed a sigh of relief at hearing that Joanne wasn't staying. I tried to think of something to say to calm the tension.

"Bitsy looks adorable, and what a beautiful sweater you have on," I finally thought to say.

"Oh, this old thing?" Joanne cooed, pleased with my comments. "Well thank you, dear. I picked it up in Morocco when Ben and I were there last summer. You wouldn't believe how inexpensive it was. Why, they just practically give things away in those third world nations!" Jill and I just looked at each other and tried not to laugh.

"Well, ta-ta, we need to run, right, itsy Bitsy." And with that, Joanne, her dog, and her cashmere sweater left. Jill and I choked into our napkins.

"Who did she think she impressed?" Jill asked. We laughed again.

"At least she gave comic relief," I answered.

"Yes, well, I'm glad she didn't stay," Jill said, finishing her crepe. I stared off for a second.

"You know," I said, "I envy her."

"What!" Jill sputtered.

"If she wanted a foster child to live with her, it would happen. If Ben actually put his foot down, she would leave and take the kid and a huge alimony settlement as well. I envy her strength, Jill."

"Looks can deceive, Robin. Joanne is more show than you think."

"That could be true. I don't really know what she's made of. But, unfortunately, I know only too well what I am made of."

"Robin, you are being too hard on yourself." I sipped my coffee and let Jill change the subject.

Lunch went on in short bursts of talk intermixed with longer silences. Jill suggested I speak to the supervisor of the Welfare Board if I felt Max's case worker wasn't doing enough. I thought that was a good idea and intended to call on Monday. It was nearing one o'clock when we paid our check and left.

Jill wanted me to go to a new boutique that just opened. I declined.

"Call me Monday and let me know what happens."

"Jill, what would I do without you?" I hugged her and she smiled.


"Guess who won again?" David said, as he put his racket away in the closet.

"Who?" I answered smiling and going to kiss him.

"You could have been married to a tennis pro. You would have cheered me at Wimbledon." I laughed.

"I'm glad you had a nice game."

"How was your beauty shop?"

"We couldn't get appointments today so we went to brunch instead, which was very nice. We ran into Joanne though , not so nice."

"I hope you were civil. We are going to the symphony with them next Saturday, Ben has tickets."

"I'm always civil," I said, with a touch of annoyance. I groaned inwardly at the thought of spending next weekend with Joanne. *Why couldn't David get enough of Ben at work and at tennis?* I thought, but I didn't say anything. David caught my tone and gave my cheek a peck as he went into the kitchen for some water.

"Well, good," he said. "I've decided how I want to spend my afternoon." He gave me that look I knew so well. I was tired, upset, and less than interested, but I smiled as we walked to the bedroom.

# Chapter 25

The rest of the weekend was spent more or less in bed. We did rouse ourselves to go to brunch Sunday morning and went to an evening movie Sunday night. David usually hated to go to movies and felt that they were idiotic and a horrific waste of time. The movie was recommended by Ben (which is why we went); a tribute to the men who fought in Korea.

David had a respect for soldiers. I'm a pacifist.

The movie was not so much a story of the Korean war, but of two families' struggle to adopt Amer-asian orphans. I saw the plight of these children, who needed to be loved, as Max. I sobbed throughout most of the movie.

Poor David, exasperated by my tears, finally said, "Let's leave, this is too much for you."

"No, no, I'm okay," I said, trying to catch my breath. David just rolled his eyes and sighed.

He put his arm around me and muttered, "This is the last time I take anyone's opinion on a movie. Though, I doubt I'll ever go to another movie again."

We drove home in silence. My thoughts were so focused on the movie that I didn't notice how tense David had become. Once home, David immediately went to get a drink. I hung up my coat and then his coat, which he had thrown on the sofa.

"Do you want something to eat?" I asked. He didn't look at me. He stared down into his drink.

He said almost awkwardly, "No, no I'm not hungry." I stared at him, unsure of this mood.

"Are you angry with me?"

He turned and looked at me. "Of course not, Robbie. Why would I be angry?" I was too emotionally drained by the movie to delve any deeper to see what was wrong.

"I think I'll take a bath. I'm kind of tired."

"Okay," David answered, absently.

I turned on the water, watching it fill the tub. I looked through my assortment of candles for something to calm myself. I settled on my favorite, apple spice. I lit two of them. I turned on the Jacuzzi jets and lowered myself slowly into the tub. I took a deep breath and closed my eyes. I began to relax. Then, I heard the door open, softly.

I didn't open my eyes. I felt David staring at me. I slowly peeked through half-closed lids. He was watching me. His eyes moved over my body, but his look was not seductive.

"May I join you?" he asked huskily. It was not that he had asked, but the way he asked, that surprised me. As if he were unsure, as if he was afraid I'd say no. I have never said no.

"Of course," I murmured. He quickly undressed. He slid under me and lifted me onto his lap. I couldn't see his face. He held me close. Very close. He held me as if he were trying to hold on to something.

"David," I said, softly.

"Shh," he replied. He laid his cheek against my hair. I knew he was upset, and I also knew I had caused it, but I said nothing. After a while, he grabbed a towel, and climbed out of the tub.

"Robin," David said, still hoarse. "Don't do this!"

"Do what?" I asked, pretending not to understand, but David had left. I cried.

# Chapter 26

I try hard to avoid confrontations of any kind. To call a supervisor to complain that one of his caseworkers was not doing his job was daunting for me. I poured a cup of coffee, took some deep breaths. I pictured Max and called.

I gave my name to the secretary who put me on hold. I panicked as my thoughts ran to voice mail, not there, or worse, will return call. How would I get through the day and keep my nerve up?

"May I help you, Mrs. Pierson?" a deep voice said.

"Yes! Yes you can!" I kept a picture of Max in my mind. I steadied my voice. "I'm very concerned about a child under the care of one of your case workers , Mr. Steve Andrews."

"What is the problem?" I went on to explain that I knew Max before he was in his present foster home, and that I was very concerned about his care in his new foster home. I mentioned the unexplained bruises and that I was being denied time to see him. He answered me in a noncommittal way.

"I'm sorry to hear this, Mrs. Pierson, but Mr. Andrews has always been a very competent social worker. I will call him and discuss your concerns and get back to you very soon."

I knew I wouldn't hear from him too soon. I had to get out. I decided to go visit my birds in the park.

I put on jeans and T-shirt and grabbed some bread. I felt as if I was suffocating and needed air. It was a breezy April day. I felt better as soon as I went outside and went walking. I started to feel better about Max. I promised myself, *After things clear up, I'll get Max to come over.*

I walked toward my hill and glanced to the playground from force of habit. I didn't see Max. I wasn't sure if this was a good sign. I climbed the hill and when I reached my bench, I plopped down. Immediately, the birds swirled overhead and landed gracefully at my feet.

"Hi sweeties," I cooed. One brave sparrow snatched a piece of bread from my hand. I held another piece carefully and he hopped back up for a moment. I finished the bread and brushed off my hands on my shorts. I took a deep breath, closed my eyes, and lay my head back. I was almost asleep when I heard a shout.

"Max, you fucking brat, get over here!" I opened my eyes to see Max, who ran quickly to the playground. Max must have been watching me, and was afraid to come over. Afraid? Why would Max be afraid of me? It didn't make sense. I jumped up and ran toward the playground. I was over the hill when I saw Max slow his steps and go reluctantly over to Tim. Tim looked angry. He glanced quickly around him. There was no one else there, only me hidden by the hill. He grabbed Max with one hand, a stick in the other. I could hear the echo of the stick as it came down on Max and broke. Max screamed loudly. I screamed also, but my scream went unheard as I watched Tim drag Max out of the park.

I froze, as I knelt on the hill. I felt the desperation of confusion. What if I would just make it worse for him? What if I couldn't get the social worker to believe what I had just witnessed?.

"Oh God, Oh God," I kept repeating as I huddled on the ground. "Why didn't Max come to me when he saw me?" Then it struck me like a lightning bolt and I fell flat on my bottom and put my face in my hands. Max thought I had abandoned him! Max probably thought I knew what was going on, that I had left him to the mercy of that fiend. *Oh, no, Maxie, you are wrong. I'll help you!* a voice inside me said. "What about David? He said to forget about Max."

*But, David didn't know Max was being abused,* I argued with myself. *When he knows the truth, he will help, Max.* I thought. I hoped. I prayed.

I ran out of the park. Max was nowhere to be seen. I hailed a taxi and went to the Child Welfare office. Once I found the office, I asked to speak to the supervisor. I waited, hands clasped. I tried to stop shaking. I took some deep calming breaths. The secretary showed me in.

Mrs. Pierson, Tom Gordon," he said shaking my hand. "Did you receive my message?"

"No, I haven't been home. I just needed to see you, I…" Mr. Gordon interrupted me.

"Please sit down, Mrs. Pierson, I've spoken with Steve. He assured me that the Westons are a wonderful family. We've never had trouble with a child in their care. As I understand it, you were offered a chance to apply as foster care parents for Max, but said you were unable to take him in."

"Yes, that's true. Mr. Gordon, I was just in Central Park and saw Max there with the eldest son of the Westons."

"Oh?"

"I don't know the details, but I saw him hit Max with a stick."

"In front of you?"

"No. He didn't see me."

"Did you call to Max? Did you ask what was going on?"

"No." I became flustered. I looked at Mr. Gordon. His eyes saw right through me. He knew who I was. He knew I knew nothing of this world, worse, that I belonged to the world of bistros and boutiques.

"Mrs. Pierson," Mr. Gordon said, with a condescending smile. "Please don't concern yourself anymore. We will take care of this little boy."

*This little boy,* I thought bitterly. *He's not Max anymore, he's just this little boy.* Anger, such as I have never felt before, exploded from within me.

"Mr. Gordon I know what I saw!" I said in a voice I didn't recognize as mine. "I have very influential friends, Mr. Gordon. I wouldn't like to see problems here because of slack leadership." Mr. Gordon's smile disappeared. Shocked, he stared at me round-eyed for a moment, but quickly recovered himself.

"On second thought," he replied slowly. "I think I need to visit the Westons myself. I will call you today, as soon as I know the full story."

"Thank you, sir. " I said shaking his hand.

"Max is lucky to have someone who cares so much," he said, smiling this time for real.

"Yes, cares from a distance," I said ruefully.

"We do what we can do, Mrs. Pierson."

I smiled weakly. I was grateful for his kind words, but I knew I could do more.

*Oh Max,* I thought. *if I can't have you, I will not rest until I make sure you're in the best home possible.* It was a good thought. I went home, my heart heavy, to wait by the telephone.

It was four o'clock when Mr. Gordon called. At first, he said, Mrs. Weston denied everything. However, when Mr. Gordon said that Tim had been seen earlier that morning at the park, Tim panicked, and the whole story came out. I was horrified by Mr. Gordon's words. It seemed that Tim and Lori were left in charge of the children on a regular basis and forced to baby-sit them.

Bob and Betty Weston used the money they received from Child Welfare to gamble. They were both addicted to gambling, and often flew on weekends to gambling casinos, leaving Tim and Lori home alone with the children.

Tim and Lori were tired of taking care of the kids. Max was the first kid he ever hurt, Tim said. He was just tired and overburdened and Max was the target for his anger.

Max was too afraid to say anything. He probably knew that Mrs. and Mr. Weston were not going to help him. *My poor Max,* I thought. *How much more do you have to suffer from misguided adults?* I felt my heart harden with resolve and my spine stiffen.

"Where is Max now?" I asked.

"All the children have been taken out of the Weston home and put in a temporary shelter. Of course, the Westons foster care license has been revoked. I'm sorry about this, Mrs. Pierson. You can be sure that this won't happen again. Any home Max and the other children will be placed in will be checked and rechecked." My thoughts were all for Max. He had to be so frightened. I heard myself interrupt Mr. Gordon.

"Yes? Did you say something, Mrs. Pierson?"

"I would like Max to stay with me instead of the temporary shelter. Also, I want to visit the home he will be placed in when you find a permanent foster home."

"I guess that could be arranged." There was a long pause as I sat holding the receiver, tightly. "Don't you need to discuss this with your husband first?" I caught the emphasis on the word "need".

"No, that will not be necessary," I said. I swallowed hard and pushed down the lump that had formed in my throat. *I must do this, I must.* I told myself, I owed it to Max.

"I'm sure my husband will be fine with the arrangement, under the circumstances," I said in my most assuring tone, "He's fond of Max."

"I'll bring Max over in the morning." I looked at the clock and saw it was six-thirty. I couldn't believe we had talked for more than two hours! I was sure Max was settled for the night. I said that would be fine.

I hung up the phone. I had taken two steps forward, but how far could I go? Not daring to further examine that question, I grabbed a bottle of wine. I had just enough time to pour a glass when David came in. He sorted the mail and then dropped it on the counter.

He noticed me with the wine in my hand. He smiled at me, surprised.

"Well, this is an unusual sight. Did you start a celebration without me?"

"It would be nice to have something to celebrate," I answered, an edge to my voice.

"Is something wrong?" I felt my lower lip begin to wobble and took a deep breath.

"David," I put down the wine glass, and hugged my arms tight around me. David started to looked worried.

"What is it, Robin?" He braced himself for bad news.

"It's Max."

"Damn it, Robin, for a second, you had me really worried."

"You should be worried!" I snapped. He stopped and stared at me. Totally shocked at my tone. Then my bravado broke. I sobbed throughout as I told the story. David led me to the sofa as I told him about the

Westons, and Mr. Gordon. I expected him to complain about my involvement. He didn't. He softly rubbed my arm, and stared straight ahead, with an almost expressionless face.

I waited until I had better control of myself before I told him that I volunteered our home, until a suitable home could be found for him. I took a deep breath.

"David," I said, shakily. He looked at me without expression. "David, I -I told Mr. Gordon that Max could stay here until they found a good foster home. I know you said I needed to ask you first, but," I hurriedly added, "I don't think it will take long, maybe just a few days." His hazel eyes started to flash.

"A few days?" he said skeptically.

"David, it will only be a few days." Then, to my total astonishment, he smiled softly.

"Okay, Robbie, I can't believe I'm doing this, but I guess I can make it through a few days. The kid's had it pretty rough." Then David's voice grew stern. "But, I'm telling you this, Robin, he better have a new home by Monday morning. Do you understand me?" His smile had vanished. I hugged David tightly.

"Of course, it will be temporary. You are wonderful, David." My strength ebbed, and I was happy for what I got.

David didn't ask if dinner was ready. He just went to the phone and ordered from Frank's. I fairly skipped into the guest room and readied it for Max. We had given all the toys and clothes I had bought him to take to the Westons. I had no idea what he would have when he arrived. I took down a couple of my old stuffed animals from the closet and put them on the bed. It didn't seem enough, but they made the room cheerier. I thought maybe I should run down to the store and pick up some clothes.

David read the Wall Street Journal. He sat in the wing chair by the fireplace.

"David, I'm going to go buy some things for Max. I'm sure he won't have much with him." David looked up in surprise. I rarely went out at night when he was home from work.

"That is ridiculous, Robin," he said, as he continued to read. "You'll have plenty of time tomorrow to buy whatever you want."

"Yes, but it would be nice to have some things for him when he arrives to make him feel welcome." David gave me another look. I quickly added, "I mean for the few days he's here." David turned the page of the newspaper.

"Robin, I really feel tomorrow is soon enough to buy out the stores. Besides, I ordered dinner, and I know you haven't eaten today." I looked down at the floor. He returned to his paper, and I let it drop. *He's probably right,* I told myself. Max can help me pick out new toys and clothes. I bet Max had grown. After-all I didn't even know what size to get him.

The doorbell rang and David went and paid for the order. "Sit down, Robbie," David said. "Look, I got your favorite, eggplant parmesan." David also had ordered Italian salad, lasagna and cannelloni for dessert. Now that I knew that Max would be here, I realized how hungry I was. I munched on a breadstick, while David poured me wine. I smiled my thanks and he smiled back.

"Hey, now save some for me," David said as he sat down.

I stuck my tongue out when I 'd finished, and then ate more. David sat and watched me. Then he began his dinner. We ate in silence. After we ate the cannelloni, I stood up and began piling the dishes.

"Boy, I'm stuffed," I said. I turned toward the kitchen. David came around in front of me, took the dishes and put them on the counter.

"The dishes are waiting," I said. David ignored my remark.

"You're mine, Robin."

"Of course, I am. Only yours," I answered, puzzled. David sighed and bent his head into my shoulder. I gently caressed his golden hair. His next words were muffled, and I strained to hear them.

"I won't share you, Robin." I looked down at him.

"I'm yours, David. Why are you saying these things?"

David kissed me. His kisses, like butterfly wings, beat against my neck. I gasped as he reached my ear, and whispered, "Never mind why. Just remember what I said."

# Chapter 27

I was up with the sun the next morning. Mr. Gordon had said he would bring Max around ten o'clock. David said little before he left for work. As he walked out the door, he said, offhandedly, "I don't want to find a toy store in here when I get home."

"You won't, David, I promise." I blew him another kiss and he smiled as he closed the door behind him.

I worked in my greenhouse until nine o'clock. After a quick shower, I sat nervously on the sofa, and absently looked at a magazine. At five minutes after ten, my nerves stretched when the buzzer rang.

"Send them up, Bill," I said, even before I heard it was Max and Mr. Gordon. I stood at the door, my hands knotted, until the knock.

Mr. Gordon held Max's hand.

"You remember Robin, right Max?" he said gently. I looked down at Max and expected a smile, but all I saw was a vacant stare. *No,* I thought, *please Max don't.* Don't what? Why should he care? He had trusted me and look where that got him. I took a deep breath and knelt down to Max.

"Hi Max," I said. He didn't respond and actually took a step backward. I fought tears.

"Why don't we go in, Max," Mr. Gordon said, as he tried to break the tension. I moved back, Mr. Gordon coaxed Max to come inside. Max kept his head down and said nothing. We sat on the sofa.

"Here are Max's things." Mr. Gordon held out a tattered bag. "I'll leave you to get reacquainted." Mr. Gordon gave me a smile of encouragement and left.

I bent down in front of Max and held his hands. He didn't pull away. His small hand sat idle in mine.

"Maxie, I know you were hurt. You have a right to be angry." He looked up at this.

"I am so sorry. I didn't know the Westons were mean. I swear I didn't know. Max, I would have never let you go to the Westons if I'd known. This won't happen again, Max. You will stay here with me until I have picked the best home a little boy can have. Maybe a house with a big yard and boys and girls to play with. Would you like that, Max?" Max said nothing. He put his head against my shoulder and I held him tight. I reassured him that everything would be alright. I tried to convince myself that it would be.

I held onto him for what seemed like forever. Max still didn't speak, but he did stop shaking. I gently pulled him off my shoulder and brushed his hair out of his eyes. The last bruise was still faint against his cheek. I softly kissed it. Max gave me a small smile.

I made Max some cinnamon toast for a snack while he looked over the guest room. I called him when it was ready and he came out carrying my old stuffed lion.

Max sat down and put the lion on the table. He took a bite of toast while I poured him some milk.

"I member that lion," he said. Those were the first words he had spoken since he came.

"You do?"I answered casually. I sat down across from him and sipped my coffee.

"Yeah, I member that dog too," he added. There was also a stuffed dog on the bed.

"You remember me telling you that they were mine when I was little?"

"No," he said, as he stuffed his mouth with toast. "I member all those new toys you got me."

"Where are those toys, Max?"

"Don't know. I had them, then they got lost."

"It's okay, Max. Let's go buy some new toys." His face brightened. I wiped cinnamon from his face.

We went to the same mall that I had taken Max to before. Max was silent in the taxi. We entered the mall, and Max tugged on my hand.

"I member this place," he said smiling, "Can I have a hamburger and French fries again?" I knelt down and hugged him.

"Of course, Max, I'll buy you anything you want." We walked hand in hand to the different clothing stores and toy stores. My arms were full when we stopped for lunch. Max held tight to the stuffed tiger I bought him. He said now the lion would have a friend. He concentrated on the hamburger and fries. Then he looked up at me.

"Member that funny game we played? You were the mommy, member?"

"Yes, I remember. That was a nice game, Max. Do you want to play it again?"

"No," he said biting his French fry. I sighed. I leaned across the table and squeezed Max's hand. He smiled, his mouth full of hamburger. I thought, *At least I'm getting smiles now.*

We made a quick stop at a grocery store. The grocery cart was piled high with mall purchases. I couldn't fit in much food, but I wanted to get something special for dinner. Max didn't know what his favorite food was so I settled on chicken. We went to the bakery counter to get some fresh bread. I noticed other young children as they sat in the front of the cart. Some of the children ate cookies, it reminded me of that day long ago when I had first seen Max.

"Number 17," the bakery assistant said. I held up my number and she took it.

"Cute little boy you've got there. Would he like a cookie?" she added. Max didn't respond.

"Of course he would," I said. "Thank you." I got my bread and Max sat in the cart munching. I wiped his face with a bit of tissue. Tears flooded my eyes, as I pushed the cart down the aisle.

Once home, I hung up Max's new clothes while he played with his blocks. I had put together the train tracks we bought and Max built a tunnel for the train to go through. I unpacked the bag that he had brought with him. Worn jeans, a sweater, and a couple of t-shirts were in it.

"Robin?" I turned around. "I hungry."

"Okay, sweetie, let's go get a snack." Max seated himself at the table.

"Do you want some crackers and cheese?"

"Could I have more that sweet toast?" he asked, hesitantly. As if he expected me to say no.

"Sure, that's a yummy snack. Why don't we both have some?"

"And milk too?"

"Coming right up." Max held his tiger close.

"You're nice, Robin."

"You're nice too, Max."

"I wish…"

"What, Max?"

"Nothing," he replied sadly. I sighed and said nothing. I would be careful this time. I wouldn't feed fantasy dreams. Dreams that wouldn't come true. Instead, I talked up all the wonderful homes that were out there. I described the nice people who would love to take care of a little boy. Max didn't seem to hear me, or maybe he didn't want to listen. I talked so that Max wouldn't ask me questions I couldn't answer.

"Robin," Max interrupted.

"Yes, Maxie?"

"I'm gonna go play now." He got off the chair and hugged his tiger tight.


David came home. The smell of roast chicken permeated the living room. He came into the kitchen with the mail. Max's train whistle went off as he came to kiss me.

"Our guest has arrived?"

"Yes, and is happily at play."

"No problems?" David asked.

"None with Mr. Gordon. Max needed warm up time." Max came into the living room. I watched him walk to David. He held onto his tiger.

"I member you," he said. David sat down on the sofa.

"I remember you," David answered, and smiled at Max.

"What's your name?"

"David. What do you have there?"

"This, my tiger. Robin got him for me."

"Wow. Why don't you come sit down and tell me what else Robin bought you. I thought I heard a train when I came home." Max smiled and sat down next to David.

"You did heard a train, my train, I made tunnels for it with blocks."

"Sounds like fun!" David replied. I couldn't believe the effort David was making to make Max feel comfortable. I hugged myself as I finished dinner.

Max seemed to enjoy the dinner. He ate heartily of the chicken, rice, and bread. He even braved a few green beans, but seemed most happy with the vanilla ice cream and chocolate syrup I picked up for desert.

"Max, who would have thought that you held the secret of getting a home-cooked dinner." David winked at me. I playfully slapped his wrist as I cleared the table. Max, of course, didn't understand, but smiled at our playfulness. He licked the last drops of chocolate off his spoon and sighed. David carried a few dishes into the kitchen and laid them in the sink. I suggested that David take Max into the den. There might be some kid show on that he'd like to watch.

"I'll see what I can find."

I heard laughter as I loaded the dishwasher. When I entered the den, I smiled. Max was laughing as he tried to explain to David what was happening in the show. From what I could make out, there was a bunch of crazy cartoon characters jumping on top of each other. Max thought it was hysterical. David tried to follow as Max explained.

"Max, after the show, do you want to go in the Jacuzzi tub?"

"What that?"

"The tub with the bubbles, you took a bath in there last time you were here." Max thought for a moment.

"Oh yea, now I member, yeah cuzzi tub." Max bounced in excitement.

"Come on, let's go," I said. I felt better. Max was comfortable now. A few hours later, I wasn't so sure anymore.

After the bath, and a few stories from the books we had bought , Max went to sleep, his arm cuddling his tiger. I was tired and went to sleep soon after. I was at the edge of a dream, when I heard a cry. I ran out of the bedroom. David, who was reading in the living room, jumped up at the scream. I ran to Max. He thrashed around in the bed crying. I held him close, and made comforting sounds. He went back to sleep. David stood in the hallway, and looked worried.

"It's alright," I said.

"What's wrong?" he asked with an edge to his voice.

"He's just been through too much for a little boy. He'll be fine now." David's look said he didn't agree. Shaking his head, he went back to his book and I went back to bed.

That night, Max had two more nightmares. David was bleary-eyed the next morning. To his credit, he went to work and he didn't say anything. Max seemed fine in the morning. He didn't mention the nightmares so I didn't say anything, either. We played in the greenhouse in the morning. I showed Max how to replant some herbs that were getting too big for their pots. We were just getting cleaned up for lunch when the phone rang.

"Hi, Mrs. Pierson. It's Tom Gordon here. I wanted to see how Max was getting along."

"We're adjusting, Mr. Gordon. Max appears to be a little more comfortable."

"Good to hear that. I hope he's not getting too comfortable, unless your plan is to keep him. We can arrange for you to become foster parents." My heart stopped.

"No, Mr. Gordon. The situation is still temporary."

"Well, in that case, I have a couple named Jacobs that would be interested in Max. They already have one foster child, a girl, and would like a little boy. They've had this little girl for six years and have shown their care to be exemplary."

"I'd like to meet them and see where they live."

"That can be arranged. They'll be out of town till Friday. How about Saturday morning? Say around eleven?"

"Okay, we'll be there." I got directions from Mr. Gordon and, I went to find Max.

Max played with his train. I sat down on the bed, and thought about what to say.

"Maxie, that was Mr. Gordon on the phone. He found some nice people named Mr. and Mrs. Jacobs that would like to meet you." Max stopped the game for a second and then resumed his train sounds.

"Max, there's another girl who lives there and Mr. Gordon said they especially wanted a little boy." Max looked up.

"When we go?"

"In a few days. It's just a visit. If we don't like the people, or if we don't think they're nice, you won't stay there, Okay?" Max didn't answer, just continued his play. "I'll go make some lunch, Max. We can go to the zoo after lunch." Max continued his train noises.

Bill gave Max a high-five as we waited for the taxi to take us to the zoo. Once there, we had a wonderful time. We stayed the afternoon. On the way home, we stopped at my plant store. I let Max pick out a pretty African violet to bring home. Next, I introduced him to Sam at the Deli.

"Hello, Mrs. Pierson, darling! Where have you been? Who's this charming young man? Here, Bubala, would you like a cookie?" Sam gave Max a black and white cookie. Max's eyes grew round at the size of it. "Sweet boy, your nephew maybe?"

"No, Sam."

"He looks good on you, sweetheart. You should have little ones with you more often." I smiled, and gave Max a quick hug.

Max helped me carry the corned beef, potato salad, and rye bread.

"This smell real good," he said.

"I'm glad. David should be home soon. You can help me set the table."

"Sure."

We put the food away and brought Max's violet out to the greenhouse. Max and I read stories and played with his toys until David came home. When we heard David open the door, Max ran out to him.

"David, David, come see what I got." Max was pulling David's arm as soon as he stepped in the doorway. I hurried over. I thought David might be angry, but to my surprise he was smiling!

"Wait, Max, let me hang up my coat." Max let go of his hand and stood as patiently as a four-and-half-year-old could. David hung up his coat as Max jumped up and down.

"Come on, come on!" David laughed.

"Okay. where are we going, Max?"

"To the plant house." David gave me a funny look. I smiled.

While Max showed David his new violet, I set the table for dinner. Max talked a blue streak as they returned from the greenhouse. David tried to make sense out of what Max said.

"Slow, down, Max. You saw a giblet at the zoo? I'm not sure I know that animal."

"It was a gazelle, Maxie," I helped.

"Oh yeah. a ga-gazelle," Max said.

"I really like gazelles," David said.

"What other aminals you like?" Max asked. David stood up and took Max's hand as he walked him over to the sofa.

"Well. I like tigers and lions…" I listened as they discussed different animals.

"Max, wash your hands for dinner, please."

"Okay," Max said. David smiled as he watched Max walk down the hallway. Then he went over to the bar to pour a drink.

"Sounds like you had a fun day," he said.

"It was very nice," I answered as I put dinner on the table. I smiled at David as he sipped his drink. His eyes had a faraway look. I knew he was thinking of his conversation with Max. "You have a way with him, David."

"Yes, well," he grunted and blushed. "Ah, corned beef, I should have guessed when I saw the new plant." I laughed. Max came bounding into the room.

"I so hungry," he stated.

"Well, let's eat then." David laughed.

David and Max played trains after dinner. At bedtime, I made up a story about a lovely fairy princess and her puppy. Max quickly fell to sleep. I said a prayer for sweet dreams and went to see David.

David sat and read the Wall Street Journal as usual. I sat quietly near him until he looked at me.

"I got a call from Mr. Gordon today," I said abruptly.

"Oh?"

"He found a home for Max. We're going to visit the Jacobs home on Saturday morning."

"Does it sound like an improvement over the last home?" David asked, while still reading the newspaper.

"Actually, it does," I answered. "But to be sure, I'm going to ask them a thousand questions."

"Do you have a plan to use thumbscrews, or are you going to put them on the rack?" David dodged as I tried to tackle him. He grabbed me roughly and then kissed me gently. We lay in each other's arm's for a while, lost in our own thoughts.


I dreamt Max was in his new home, and he called for me. I kept hearing my name over and over. Then I woke and realized Max really was screaming my name. I jumped up. David woke as well.

"Not again," he mumbled.

"Go to sleep, David. I'll take care of him." I ran to the guest room. Max was sitting up and screaming as he clutched his tiger.

"Maxie, sweetie it's okay, Robin's here." Max held on to me, his fingers tight around my neck. I held him close. Slowly, his grip relaxed and he fell back to sleep. Twice more, he woke up shrieking. When I returned to bed, David had his arm over his eyes.

"What's going on in there?" he grunted.

"It's okay, David, go back to sleep."

"It's not okay. I'm tired. You're tired. This is not what I bargained for when I said a few days." I was suddenly afraid David would say Max had to go.

"David, he's been through a lot, please. I'll take care of him."

"Fine," he snapped. He turned over and went back to sleep.

# Chapter 28

Thursday and Friday passed quickly. Max woke only once on Thursday night, but Friday night held multiple awakenings. Both David and I were tired. David was extremely edgy.

I listened in bed to David slam things around in the kitchen. I could tell by the slams that his mood would last the day. *David, patience,* I wanted to scream. He knew what Max has been through. *As usual, all he could think about was himself,* I grumbled to myself. Then I heard Max speak.

"Hi David, what you making?"

"Coffee," David answered shortly.

"Oh, what's wrong?" Max asked. David calmed his voice.

"Nothing, Max. I'm just a little tired."

"I sorry I was loud last night. I had bad dreams." Silence for a moment and then David answered.

"Max, don't be sorry. Everyone has bad dreams now and then."

"Yea? You too?" Max sounded so surprised that David laughed. I slipped on my robe and walked to the door of the bedroom. I peaked out and saw David bend down to Max. Then, to my surprise, he picked Max up, and walked to the living room. He sat down on the wing chair and held Max in his lap.

"You, know, once when I was little…" David started to say. Max interrupted him.

"Little like me?" David hugged him.

"Just like you, I used to dream about monsters. Big hairy ones with sharp teeth and big claws."

"What happen when a monster come?"

"It would scare me and I'd scream and cry. My mom would come and hold me until I stopped, then I'd fall back to sleep."

"Then you have a good dream?"

"Sometimes. Sometimes I'd have the same dream again and wake up and cry. Once for a whole week, every night, I had that monster dream."

"Every night?" Max exclaimed. David hugged him closer, and then kissed his hair.

"What you do?" Max asked.

"Well, one night, my dad came in the room, and you know what he said?"

"No, what?"

"He said, "I've had enough of this monster that keeps bothering my little boy. I'm going to sit on this bed. If that monster so much as makes a peep in this room, I'm going to open the window and throw it so far that he will never find his way back to this house again." I fell back to sleep with my dad sitting on my bed. As soon as I started to thrash around, my dad figured the monster was back and said into my ear as I slept, "David, David, I've grabbed that monster by the arm. I have him at the window and I'll throw him outside." Dad said that as soon as he told me he threw the monster out the window, I smiled. I slept through that whole night with a smile on my face."

"How'd he know you smile all night?"

"Because Dad sat on my bed all night and watched me. And you know what else?" David continued, "I never had another monster dream again."

"Wow, dads are sure strong." Max gave a sad sigh.

"Come, Max, let me get you some breakfast," David said, softly.

Max hopped off David's lap and walked slowly to the kitchen. He sat down at the table and David went to get him juice. I walked in yawning. I tried to act like I'd just woken up and hadn't heard anything.

"Good morning, guys." I kissed both of them on the cheek. David smiled at me as he poured Max some cereal.

"Robin, David told me how to scare monsters away."

"Really! That's great. Can I help you scare them?"

"No, you need a dad," Max said, sadly. David busied himself with the milk.

"Let me try, Max. I've been known to scare a few monsters in my time." Max looked skeptical.

"Well, okay."

David left to play tennis and Max and I got ready to meet the Jacobs. Bill had the taxi waiting for us when we got downstairs. Max was quiet on the way over. I tried to relax him and convince him that this was just a visit. I talked about things we could do after we left the Jacobs. To all my suggestions, Max just answered, "Don't care." I told him we'd talk about it more after our visit.

It took about twenty minutes to reach the Jacobs. I told Max that we were so close that I could visit often. Max said nothing. I sighed, thinking that I probably wouldn't see Max at Central Park too often. I gave myself a shake and plastered a smile on my face. The taxi pulled up in front of a duplex with a small lawn and lovely flowers in front.

I saw Mr. Gordon's car in front of the taxi. I paid the taxi driver and helped Max out. I saw children that were a little older than Max next door. I pointed out the children to Max. He eyed them, warily.

We rang the doorbell. As we waited, I heard a television, and a little girl laughing as she watched Saturday morning cartoons. A pretty woman who looked to be in her early thirties answered the door. She smiled at me and then turned to Max. Max took a step back squeezing my hand tight.

"Hi, Max," she said softly, "I'm Terry. I've been waiting to meet you."

Suddenly, a small dog came bounding in. She barked and came right over to Max and danced in front of him, eager to be petted. Max laughed and let go of my hand. He tried to pet the dog and the dog kissed him on the nose. Max squealed in delight.

"Hi puppy! Hi puppy!" he kept repeating. Terry smiled.

"The welcome wagon has arrived," Terry said. "I really should have Muffin make all the greetings, right Muffy?" Terry patted Muffin's head and then held her hand out to shake mine.

"It's nice to meet you, Robin, come in. I have coffee made." Max was already on the floor of the living room playing with Muffin and her pull toy. The little girl sat on the couch and watched television.

"Max, this is Kimmi. She's been waiting to meet you," Terry said.

"Hi, Max," Kimmi said shyly. Max looked at Kimmi. She was a tiny little girl.

"You got any real big boys here?" Max asked Terry as he looked warily around.

"No, just Kimmi." Max sighed visibly in relief. Terry, who knew what happened at the Westons, looked at me sadly. I blinked back tears.

I noticed the toys stacked in bins against the walls. The couch Kimmi sat on and the armchair next to it were worn, but looked like they had seen a lot of bouncing and cuddling.

Two bookshelves stood next to the television stand, and held a mix of children's and adult books.

"There are cookies in the kitchen if you both want a snack," Terry said to the children. We walked into the kitchen and let them get acquainted.

Mr. Gordon sat at the table talking with a man who also seemed to be in his thirties. He had dark hair, and a friendly smile.

Mr. Gordon introduced us. Phil Jacobs stood and shook my hand. Terry poured coffee. I glanced out the back window and saw a yard with a swing set and a sandbox. Mr. Gordon caught my glance.

"Everything a child could want," he said and grinned.

"Terry likes to keep toy stores in business," Phil said in a light-hearted way. "Look who's talking. Do I have something hiding behind my chair?" Just then Kimmi and Max ran in, followed closely by Muffin.

"Mommy, Mommy, Max and I want a cookie."

"Go sit down and I'll get you both some milk."

Phil saw Max and said, "Hey, buddy." Phil looked at Mr. Gordon." I think you sent us a future football player." Max looked confused, but smiled at Phil. Max walked to my chair. Phil reached behind his chair and brought out a big wrapped present.

"This is for you Max," Phil said.

"Wow!" Max said. He promptly tore off the wrapping. It was a big, gray truck with a remote control attached to it. Phil showed Max how to drive the car with the remote.

We stayed for almost two hours. Terry showed us the upstairs room Max would be in if he stayed. (Mr. Gordon had explained what had happened to Max at the last home. He also told them how I fitted into the picture). The room was painted a light blue. There was a twin bed with a sports comforter spread on top. There was a football lamp and matching bookcase with some children's books already in it. There were also some stuffed animals high on shelves over the bed. I was pleased. It looked like a good home.

Terry was with the children in the living room and helped Max with his truck. I asked Phil if I could use his phone to call for a taxi.

"No need, Mrs. Pierson, I'm going back to my office. I have some paperwork to do before I can begin my weekend. I'll be glad to drop both you and Max off," Mr. Gordon said as he stood up. I went to get Max. I stopped in the doorway and watched. Terry was driving the car, making it chase Muffin. Muffin yapped at the car and the kids were laughing.

"Mommy, show Max how it goes backwards," Kimmi said. Terry began to take Max's hand to move the remote.

"How come she call you mommy?" Max asked suddenly. Terry put her arm around Max.

"Kimmi's been living here a long time, since she was a baby. Maybe when you have lived here a while, you'll want to call me Mommy, too. I would love that, Max." Max smiled and looked at the car. I felt my heart break a little more.

Mr. Gordon asked how I felt about the Jacobs on the way home. I said I was very pleased. I tried to look pleased. I found it hard to keep my voice from cracking. Max chatted happily about the house and the Jacobs. He held his truck, tightly. He told Mr. Gordon that he was going to bring it with him when he went back to see the Jacobs.

"I think we have a winner here," Mr. Gordon said to me. I agreed. Mr. Gordon dropped us off at my home. Max bounded ahead to show Bill his new truck. Mr. Gordon held me back a moment.

"Should I come for Max on Monday morning?"

I tried to smile. I forced out a "yes." Then I added, "I think the Jacobs will make wonderful foster parents. You did tell them I'd like to visit Max?"

"Yes, and they were fine with that. The Jacobs' philosophy is that the more people a child can have to love them, the better." I sighed. Mr. Gordon looked at me,

"You are doing the right think, Mrs. Pierson. Raising a child is a tough job. Raising someone else's child is especially difficult. You need both parents to be completely supportive and committed. Max deserves that much."

"Max will be ready Monday," I answered. Mr. Gordon smiled and left.

# Chapter 29

Max held my hand in the elevator. He chatted about the morning, Kimmi, and all she told him. The elevator stopped at my penthouse. I opened the door and Max immediately went to put his truck with his other toys. I stood and looked at my white leather couch and matching wing chairs. I saw the white carpet and glass tables as if for the first time.

I walked through the living room and looked out the patio door. The only things green out there were my plants in the greenhouse. Max called me. I walked down the hallway toward the guestroom.

David came home from his tennis game. I cleaned up a late lunch. Max played with his toys and watched television in the den.

"How was the morning?" David asked as he gave me a peck on the cheek.

"Terrible," I answered. David looked at me. "The Jacobs are wonderful. They have the most perfect house for children, and they seemed the most loving of people. I couldn't pick a better family for Max."

"Terrible?" David asked, not understanding. I sighed and put the last dish in the dishwasher.

"There is no terrible part. I'm just sad about losing him."

"Robin," David said sternly. "You aren't getting any ideas, are you?"

"No! I'm just sad. I can be sad, can't I?" My voice broke and I took a hard swallow. David put his hands on my shoulders and gave me a squeeze.

"Yes, you can be sad. Hey, how about I call the travel agent Monday and we plan a weekend cruise," David said. "We can go on that new state of the art luxury cruise liner. Very exclusive, no more than a handful of people." I nodded, not trusting myself to speak. David hugged me.

"We couldn't do trips like that with kids," David continued. "Christ, we'd have to spend all our vacations at Disney World."

I didn't say anything, but I thought, *Disney World would be nice.*

Max came into the kitchen. David swooped down and picked Max up.

"Hey, I heard you met a great family today."

"Yea! They had a dog and I got a truck and..." David carried Max to the sofa and sat down with him on his lap, listening to the retelling of the morning events. I gave myself a mental shake. I was going to make these last two days wonderful. I'd have plenty of time to be sad, later.

"So what shall we do this afternoon, Max?" David asked.

"Um, don't know." Max answered. I came over and sat down next to them "We could take a ride on the Staten Island ferry, see the Statue of Liberty," I said.

"That sounds great," David said. Max bounced up and down on David's lap.

"We gonna take a fairy ride in the sky?" We both laughed.

"The Staten Island ferry, honey, that's a boat. Not the kind of fairies that have wings."

"Oh a boat, that still fun," Max said, clapping his hands.

"Let's go," David said.

We got to Battery Park just in time for the next departure. Once aboard, we saw it was very crowded with tourists. Max held my hand and jumped to try and see over the people. David picked him up and sat him on his shoulders. I stared at them for a moment. They looked so much alike. As if reading my mind, an older lady stopped and smiled at Max, who was laughing at the gulls swooping overhead.

"My, what an adorable child," she said. "It's always so nice to see a father and son that resemble each other so closely. It just makes such a pretty picture." Max didn't pay much attention to the woman's comments. He was too busy watching the gulls. David blushed, and was about to say something when I jumped in.

"Thanks," I said. The lady smiled and moved on. David raised his eyebrows at me and I shrugged.

"Why spoil this woman's kind words?" I said. David didn't say anything. Although it seemed to me, he hugged Max tighter.

At the Statue of Liberty, we stayed on the outside, and walked around. We both felt it would be too much of a climb for Max. He was content to run around, and point to the statue in awe. We went into the gift shop and bought Max a cap and a little Statue of Liberty souvenir. He also liked one of those snowballs with the statue inside. He enjoyed shaking it to see the snow fall down. David found a Frisbee with the Statue of Liberty on it, and after paying for everything, we went outside to show Max how to throw it.

I sat back on my elbows to watch them. They were cute. I was impressed with David's patience. Not something I usually saw. Max kept throwing it every which way until he threw it straight in the air. It bonked David on the head when it came down. I thought David would lose it then, but seeing how upset Max looked at what he did, David smiled and knelt down and told him it was fine. Max reached over to David's forehead and rubbed his hand over the sore spot. David swooped Max in the air and spun him around. They ended up on the ground tackling each other. I laughed so hard, tears were in my eyes.

They both stopped to look at me. David whispered something to Max. Then, before I knew it, they both tackled me. David tickled me while I tried to put grass down his shirt. I put grass down Max's shirt and he giggled as he tried to get it out. We rested on the grass exhausted. Finally, David said, "We'd better head back."

We stopped on the way home at an Italian restaurant. Max behaved very well. He chatted about the Statue of Liberty as he ate spaghetti and meatballs. David answered Max's questions readily. He seemed relaxed. David had really made this a great day for Max. He didn't even seem to mind spending his Saturday night with a four-year-old. It made me love him more than ever.

Max fell asleep in the back seat of the car as we drove home. David carried him inside. I got him ready for bed. I carefully wiped the last of the grass out of his hair.

"Good night, Max," I whispered.

"Good night, Robin Mommy." Max said sleepily. My heart contracted as I pulled the covers up over his shoulders.

I came into the living room where David was having a brandy. I came behind him and started rubbing his shoulders. He smiled at me and closed his eyes.

"MMM, don't stop, that feels fabulous. That little kid gave me quite a workout today."

"You were wonderful with him, David. I can't believe how sweet you were to Max." David put his brandy glass on the table and pulled me over his shoulder and onto his lap. He kissed me deeply and I snuggled into him. He rubbed my back gently,

"Max is a nice kid and I'm glad he's finally going to be part of a good family."

"Me too," I said faintly.

"Now, I think I need a little more practice in my tackling maneuver," David said. I laughed. David picked me up and carried me into the bedroom. He tossed me onto the bed, and spoke, smiling. "Prepare to go down."

Max had been asleep for about three hours and there had been no nightmares. I guess he was exhausted or happy enough to banish monsters. *Robin Mommy,* I thought as I felt my throat tighten. I gave myself a little shake. *Stop that,* I told myself, *I want him to be with the Jacobs they are wonderful people.* You will go visit him and take him out for day trips. A true Auntie Robin. *But I don't want to be Auntie Robin,* I argued with myself. *I want to be Robin Mommy.* Stop it. I gave myself another shake.

"What are you doing? You're not getting sick, are you? You keep shaking," David said irritably.

Embarrassed, I lied, "No, no I'm just cold." David threw the afghan at me, turned over and fell asleep. I shut out any other thoughts and fell asleep.

I awoke startled. It was still dark with just the light from the night light in the hall bathroom shining through the door. I looked at David's alarm clock. It was four o'clock in the morning. I lay still, listening for Max but didn't hear a sound. Then I heard a soft grumbling. I turned on my pillow and looked at David. He was thrashing about, talking in his sleep. "No," he cried. I gently reached out to his shoulder and patted it. He quieted down and fell into a deeper sleep. I stared up from my pillow, looking at the ceiling for a long time.

I heard a crash and a stifled giggle as I awakened. Bright sunlight filled the room. I looked at the clock, it was ten thirty. I heard another giggle. I looked over and saw the other side of the bed empty. *Well, I guess everyone's up,* I thought.

I grabbed my robe and walked to the bedroom doorway. Max was sitting at the table trying to peel an orange. David was hopping about trying to make pancakes, fry bacon, and make coffee all at the same time.

"Sleeping beauty awakens," David said, as I entered the kitchen. "I thought you might sleep the day away."

"How could I with those delicious smells drifting into the bedroom?" David grinned at my response, well pleased with himself.

"Hi Robin Mommy." David lifted his eyebrows at this, but I ignored him.

"Good morning, Maxie Max. You are doing a great job with that orange." Max smiled at me while trying to suck the juice that dripped down his arm. I gave David a kiss.

"Can I help?"

"Now you ask. The work's all done."

"Is there a better time to ask?"

David laughed and slapped my bottom. "Go, lazy, sit and appreciate all I do for you."

"I always do," I said. This was a rare treat for David to cook breakfast.

Max helped me with the dishes after the breakfast. We carefully loaded them in the dishwasher as David sat in the living room and read the Sunday paper. I got Max dressed.

Max ran into the living room and jumped on David's lap, crumbling his paper. David didn't get angry. I thought, sadly, *The last day, David is making allowances.*

"What do you want?" David said to Max, tickling him. Max laughed.

"I thought I'd take Max to the park and let you relax and finish your paper, David." Then he surprised me again.

"No, no I'll come too. We need to get some more Frisbee lessons in, don't we, Max?"

"Yeah, you come," Max answered, excitedly.

An hour later, we were headed to Central Park. Max bounced happily along as he held my hand. I had bread for the birds in the other hand and David held the Frisbee.

At the entrance to the park was a mime. She was comically dressed. She stood high on a box with her white face frozen. Max stared at her with his mouth open. I nudged David to give her some money. He gave me his, 'Are you crazy' look. He glared at me as I put five dollars in her flowered painted can.

The mime smiled down at Max. Max stepped back and clutched my hand harder. Then the mine put her hand in her pants pocket. She pulled it out and it was empty. Putting on a confused face, she thrust her hand deeper in her pocket and rummaged around for a second. A small crowd gathered around us. I looked down at Max's look of awe. I felt David breathe out in exasperation. The mime again pulled out nothing. She cried silent tears and then stopped. Her face lit up as if she had an idea. She stepped toward Max and pretended to take something from his ear. Max looked at her as she rubbed her gloved hands together. She again thrust her hand into her pocket and pulled out a folded pink paper. She opened it up and it was a heart, which she handed to Max, blowing him a kiss before she refroze herself on the box.

The crowd clapped. Max smiled brightly at his heart. David said, "Oh please," under his breath. I ignored David and smiled down at Max, who now pretended he was a mime as we made our way into Central Park.

We walked toward the playground. Max let go of my hand and ran toward the monkey bars. The playground was crowded and all the benches were taken. David and I stood by the monkey bars and watched Max climb.

"Look at him go," David said. I watched as Max got to the top rung and began tight-roping across. David stepped forward as if to go after him. I held his arm.

"He's okay." I remembered back to that day when I first saw Max climb the monkey bars. Could it really be eight months ago? It seemed like yesterday. David almost stepped forward again when Max swung down and caught the bar with the ease of a gymnast.

"Wow, he's great," David said, impressed.

*He sure is,* I thought.

So much of the day brought back memories. We watched Max play in the sandbox and swing on the swings. I thought about Halloween when he had been the only child without a costume. *That won't happen at the Jacobs,* I told myself. We went to feed the birds and Max happily tossed bread to them. It was a warm day, not like that freezing day when I handed Max my sweatshirt. So many memories.

David and Max played Frisbee. Max had improved. At least David didn't get hit on the head. The chimes of the ice cream truck rang through the park. Max didn't stop his play, like the other children. He didn't know what the music meant. David caught the Frisbee. He went to Max. He explained that the truck sold ice cream and asked Max if he'd like some. He took Max's hand and led him to the truck. A crowd formed around the truck. We waited until it was our turn.

"What would you like, Max?" David asked. Max studied images on the truck of all the different ice cream choices.

"That one." Max pointed at a red, white, and blue Popsicle.

David and I had ice cream also. I grabbed a lot of napkins.

We found a bench near the hill and Max sat down and happily slurped away. I tried to catch his drips and then finally gave up on the futile effort. David, usually Mr. Clean, said, "Let him be, we'll wash him when we get home." I looked at him surprised. David shrugged and gave me an impish grin.

We left the park after our ice cream. David carried Max the last part of the way home. It was comical watching David. He tried to make sure that Max's sticky shirt didn't touch his clean one.

# Chapter 30

I put Max in the bathtub an soon as we got home. He wanted to go in the Jacuzzi tub. He sat and watched the bubbles swirl around him as I washed the stickiness off him. "How did you get your legs sticky? That must have been a super drippy pop." Max giggled.

"It was, I liked it."

"I could tell." Max moved his boat along the water and watched the bubbles push it this way and that.

"Robin?"

"Yes?"

"Do Terry have a cuzzi tub too?"

"I don't think so, Max." I wiped his ears with a washcloth.

"Robin?"

"MMM?"

"Do Terry live by the park?" I sat back on my heels.

"Not by the park that we were at today. She has other parks near her, I'm sure. You'll have a swing set right in the back yard so you won't have to go to the park. You can swing whenever you want."

"But I like the park," he said.

"I'm sure Terry will take you to the park, Max. And you'll have Kimmi to play with too."

"And Muffin?"

"Maybe Muffin can go to the park too," I answered. Max continued to watch his boat as I watched him.

"Robin?"

"What?"

"You come bisit me?"

"Of course, Max."

"And David?"

"We'll both come and take you out for the day."

"Really come?" Max asked, anxiously. I hugged him tightly.

"Max, the Jacobs are great. They are going to be the mommy and daddy that you always wanted, and you even get a sister and a dog."

"You not be Robin Mommy anymore," he said sadly.

"No, Max," I said, swallowing my tears. Then I added with false cheerfulness. "I know, let's pretend that I'm the Auntie and you're my nephew. When I come and visit, you can call me Auntie Robin and David, Uncle David. You want to call me Auntie Robin now?"

"No, you be Robin Mommy till 'morrow."

"Okay Max," I said with a catch in my throat. I helped him out of the bath and dressed him in clean clothes.

David was in his office working his portfolio, when Max and I came out of the guest room. Max went into the office and sat on the brown leather wing chair.

"Max, you want me to read you a story?" I asked.

"No, I watch David." David smiled at Max.

"It's pretty boring, but okay, Max."

I left them and went into the kitchen. I made a fresh pot of coffee. I was listening to it brew when the phone rang. It was Mr. Gordon.

"Hi, Mrs. Pierson, I'm just calling to see if everything's okay for tomorrow?"

"Yes, we will be ready."

"I'll be there at eight. I'm sorry about the early time, but I have to go out of town at eleven and I want to see this personally settled before I leave. Is Max excited?" Mr. Gordon asked.

"Yes, I think so, and a little nervous."

"Well, that's to be expected. Okay, then, I'll see you tomorrow." I hung up the phone and poured the coffee. David and Max came into the kitchen.

"Who was that?" David asked.

"It was Mr. Gordon. He wanted to tell me he'll be here at eight to get Max and take him to the Jacobs."

"Oh," David said.

"Why don't you come?" Max asked.

"I can't, Max. But you know Mr. Gordon. He'll see you safely settled. You can call me when you get there, okay?"

"Okay," Max murmured.

I made a chicken and potato dish for dinner but no one was hungry. David absently twirled the wine in his glass and Max took small bites of potato. I took two bites of salad and put my fork down. I couldn't get anything past the lump in my throat.

David helped me clean up. Max watched television. We made light conversation. I didn't think I could bear it if David mentioned the trips we could go on, or what we could do without a "kid" in the house. Thankfully, he said nothing. After putting the last dish in the sink, David went to sit with Max. I joined them. Max laughed a little at the show, but the screen could have been blank for all that I saw.

Max fell asleep against David's shoulder. However, we still didn't move. Finally, I got up and took Max and put him to bed. I slipped his pajamas on so as not to wake him. I stood and watched him a long time. Max's even breathing was the only sound in the room. David came in and put his arm around me.

He took me to the bedroom. He started to kiss me on my neck until he reached my lips. For once though, I couldn't respond. He looked into my eyes and I fought to keep the tears back. He sighed and held me close. We lay next to each other, fully dressed. I soon fell asleep.

The night was full of dreams. My mind jumped from one scene to another. In all my dreams, Max was in danger. I couldn't get to him. I would try to reach him and then the dream would shift and he was in a new state of peril. At one point, I heard him cry louder than the dream. I woke, but the apartment was quiet. I didn't feel David near me, but was asleep before I had time to think of where he was.

I slept fitfully, when I woke again, it was still dark. I looked over to see the time and saw that David wasn't in bed. It was three a.m. I crept silently to the guest room. There was David sitting on Max's bed. He still had his clothes on. He must not have gone to sleep when he heard Max cry out. Max was sound asleep now. There was even a little smile on his face.

"David," I whispered, "I'm so sorry. Why didn't you wake me when he cried?" David put his arm around me and squeezed me gently. "Shh, it's okay. I needed to throw a monster out the window."

We were all up early the next morning. I had Max's bag packed and at the door at seven o'clock. We ate breakfast together. David was dressed for work and would leave after Max did. David tried to be cheerful. He teased Max about what it would mean to have a sister.

"Now remember," David said, "older sisters can be bossy. Don't let her boss you around too much."

"How you know they bossy, you have one?"

"Well, no, but I had a lot of friends that did."

"Oh!" Max replied. I said nothing. It was hard enough to keep from crying, let alone talk too. At eight o'clock sharp, the buzzer rang. David told Bill to send Mr. Gordon up.

I put a light jacket on Max, since the morning was chilly. He clutched his tiger in one hand and his truck in the other. David let Mr. Gordon in and shook his hand.

"Well, Max," he said. "Are you ready to go?" Max didn't answer.

"You come see me, right?" Max asked in a whisper.

"Yes, Max, we will," I replied hoarsely.

"I promise, Max, David and Robin will come visit. Nobody will stop them," Mr. Gordon said. Max turned to David.

"Bye, David," Max said, bravely.

"Bye, Max, we'll see you soon," David said as he hugged him. Max came back to stand in front of me. I zipped up his jacket.

"Bye, Robin Mommy." I hugged Max tightly and took a deep breath, breathing in the scent of him.

"I'll see you soon, Max," I managed to whisper. Max turned and walked toward Mr. Gordon. I bit my lip to keep the tears back. Suddenly, Max dropped his tiger and truck and threw himself at me.

He cried and screamed, "No, Mommy, please, Max stay, please Max stay!" I tried to reassure him, but couldn't get the words out. I couldn't stop the tears from streaming down my face. David stood, not meeting my gaze.

"It's okay, Max, you'll see them soon. Be a big boy, Max, it's okay," Mr. Gordon said, as he tried to pry Max off me.

"No! He doesn't have to be a big boy," David said gruffly. Shocked, I looked up at David through tear-filled eyes. He took a deep breath.

"It's not okay, Mr. Gordon." We all stared at David, but he only looked at Max. Their eyes locked. "Tell the Jacobs we're sorry, but Max is staying here."

Mr. Gordon stepped back from Max.

"Are you sure, Mr. Pierson?"

"Yes, I am sure."

"That's fine, Mr. Pierson, that's more than fine," Mr. Gordon said, and smiled. "And don't worry about the Jacobs. Unfortunately, there are lots of little boys that need good homes. There will be someone else for the Jacobs. Actually, I would say today is a blessing. I can place two children at one time." Mr. Gordon winked at me. I stared at him. My shock and happiness had left me speechless. Mr. Gordon opened the door and let himself out. I squeezed Max. Max hugged me then ran to David. David picked him up and came over to me.

"I guess I can learn to share you," he whispered to me.

"David," I said, touching his arm. "You won't have to share me, but you will have to share Max." He laughed. We hugged each other tightly, as my tears of happiness wet all our faces.

www.ingramcontent.com/pod-product-compliance
Lightning Source LLC
Chambersburg PA
CBHW020558250626
47154CB00004B/1266